Faded Letters

Faded Letters

MAURIZIO ASCARI

Patrician Press ● Manningtree

Maurizio Ascari is a senior lecturer and researcher in English Literature at Bologna University. He has had many articles and books on English-language writers published, including Henry James and Katherine Mansfield, and his book, *A Counter-History of Crime Fiction* was short-listed in the 'Best Critical/Biographical' category for the Mystery Writers of America's Edgar Awards. *Faded Letters* is his first creative work.

Published by Patrician Press 2013.
For more information: www.patricianpress.com

First published as a paperback edition by Patrician Press 2013
E-book edition published by Patrician Press 2013

British Library Cataloguing in Publication Data. A catalogue
record for this book is available from the British Library.

ISBN 978-0-9927235-2-1

Printed and bound in Peterborough by Printondemand-worldwide

www.patricianpress.com

We are but hollow vessels, washed through by history.

Everything is chance or nothing is chance.
If I believed the first I would be unable to live on, but I am not
yet fully convinced of the second.

Etty Hillesum, 15th June 1941

Last night I wrote a sentence on a piece of paper. I filled the sink with water. I dipped the paper in the water and went to sleep. This morning the paper was there but the sentence was gone. Only faded letters, blanks. The soaking wet paper broke up as soon as I tried to lift it. Thus began this book. Only faded letters, blanks. A story that had been written in a distant past needed to be rewritten. And in the meantime what I held in my hands was that drowned, fragile paper, a page that had been deleted.

What I heard were only echoes and I knew that starting from those echoes I had to conjure up the voices of the dead, noises that were no longer, music that had stopped playing long ago. Only my imagination could lead me where documents and memories failed. Only a novel could give life to what time had wiped out. I was aiming for a different kind of reality, the reality of vision. I felt responsible, I was afraid, but I could not help responding. Somebody was knocking on the door and I got up to open it.

Zwangsarbeit

1st March 1944, Novara.

Antonio's wife could not accompany him to the platform. It was a military train. Pina had hugged him before he went to the police station and was taken into custody.

While waiting for the train, Antonio held time back with all his strength, striving to stop it, clinging to the present that was turning into past, dreading the future that was turning into present.

It was useless. He was no longer there. Already the city was no longer his.

They were made to line up with their bags at their side, those humiliated men, sad with a sadness so deep that he felt utterly empty.

He fixed his eyes on the concrete floor. Near his feet one tile was missing. In that pool of dark water a cigarette floated.

2nd March 1944, Novara.

Pina sat down at the kitchen table. She had no more tears to cry. It had all happened so quickly... She did not want the coffee that her mother was handing her. Although she knew it would do her good. Duty required her to write that letter. Perhaps she would find a little comfort by sharing her pain with her mother-in-law.

> *Dear Mother,*
>
> *I believe you have already received the letter in which Antonio announced his departure for Germany. One day has already gone by: forgive me for not writing immediately but I hope you will understand my state of mind.*
>
> *The whole thing was so sudden: you know, on Saturday morning Antonio received a postcard inviting him to go to the German Command to be enlisted for the German front. When he presented the document to his company he was reassured. He could not be conscripted being the holder of an exemption granted by the Fabbriguerra Ministry. Not only was the factory where he worked "protected", being in the service of the Germans, but his presence was reputed to be indispensable.*
>
> *Having obtained these explanations, Antonio felt reassured. On Monday morning, however, he was asked to go to the Command, where he was examined, declared able and enlisted as a textile technician. He will be sent to Germany, hopefully to a cotton mill, the name and location of which we do not know yet.*
>
> *All this information is given in advance to those who volunteer, but since Antonio was forced to accept an unwanted place he was not told anything.*
>
> *I leave you to imagine our dismay and his! Our house is empty and without sun: my mother feels like a wretch and only today am I beginning to come to terms with what has happened.*
>
> *I cannot hide the fact that our days are desolate and terrible.*
>
> *Remember us in your prayers, Antonio for his salvation and for me to be a little more resigned.*
>
> *Affectionate greetings, Pina*

NB You must know that this recruitment has so far occurred only in Novara and Vercelli, in the latter city for women as well. Hostages?

31st March 1944, Novara.

The Office of Placement clerk finished smoking his cigarette. It was time to return to his desk. He did not feel like working, however. He thought of the young people who at that time were on some mountain, with a rifle on their shoulder.

He wondered what a partisan's life was like. He would never make it there. It was the Americans who should change things. Only they had the strength to beat the Axis.

Even if he did not show it, he was waiting for the day when the first Jeep carrying a Stars and Stripes flag would enter Novara. It would happen sooner or later. He was certain of it. You had only to wait.

He sat down at his desk.

"Is the report ready?" asked the office head.

"I'm typing it."

"Good. So I can sign it. It must be sent today. Is that clear?"

The clerk took a blank sheet of paper, carbon paper and another sheet. He put them in his typewriter and the clicking of keys began:

REPORT CONCERNING THE ENLISTMENT OF WORKERS FOR GERMANY, FOR THE MILITARY INSPECTORATE OF LABOUR AND FOR THE TODT ORGANISATION.

In relation to your telegram dated 22nd March we inform you that in accordance with current regulations on 15th February the census of the residents in the city of Novara born between 1899 and 1926 began by means of a draft card.

The work is carried out according to the following criteria:

Employees of the Provincial Placement Office are working at the local Town Hall to compile the lists of citizens who must be conscripted.

Once they have been conscripted, a special commission examines, on the production of relevant documents, their social and family position. If they are deemed suitable they are immediately subjected to medical examination and assigned to work in Germany, at the Military Inspectorate of Labour and at the Todt Organisation.

The result so far is not negligible as between volunteers and conscripted parties as many as 625 men and 100 women have left. Another 155 men and 11 women are also ready for expatriation, while 80 workers were assigned to the Inspectorate of Labour.

The main result of the census has not yet been achieved, because those who have turned up so far were for various reasons those most likely to be disregarded (physical defects, employed in protected factories, etc.). The majority has almost totally failed to report so far. Yet, it was decided to send the list of their names to the police for the competence measures.

Done. Another hour and the day was over. He saw himself sitting at the café with his friends. Of course those poor people who had been taken away... Luckily, he did not know a single one.

Kinderszenen

23rd July 1905, Loiano.

It was Umberto's first child. Born in the middle of the night. He would call him Antonio, like his elder brother. Nine pounds. A big boy! He would walk to the café in the square and pay for a round of drinks.

He thought back to the day when – as he was looking for antique furniture in the Apennines – he had met Maria, who could almost be his daughter. He had wanted her. And she had accepted him because he was tall and well made, with a nice upturned moustache.

Maria was in the big bed, exhausted. She had been told so many times that childbirth is painful. As long as it does not happen, however, you do not know.

She had been drinking the soup that Benizia (her mother) had lovingly brought her: "You have to drink it, Maria. Go on. It'll do you good. You don't want to get sick, do you?"

She had accepted her husband's kiss, his gratitude, but now she wanted to be alone.

She would send the child out to a wet nurse. There was no way she could give him all that milk. He was a plump little animal, a red piglet. It was not that she didn't love him. When he was inside her she used to talk to him. But now she was too tired.

She tried to sleep, but her head was swimming in a sea of thoughts. Her honeymoon in Rome. The churches, the squares... The photo that was on the dresser.

And her first pain when Umberto had told her: "I have an illegitimate child. I didn't want to acknowledge him, but I gave his mother some money to raise him." Some money... A shiver struck her body like a laugh.

13th February 1907, Loiano.

Maria was pregnant again. At first she struggled between nausea and dizziness. Then she got better. If it was a girl she would call her Veronica.

She did not want another boy. They made too much noise, boys. A little girl instead...

She thought of the booties that she would crochet. White, with ribbons of various colours. She would arrange them all in a row on the dresser. And the clothes. And the bonnets. She would dress her like a doll. She inhaled the smell of her skin while she was giving her a kiss on the forehead.

12th March 1910, Loiano.

Progress had reached the Apennines. The Italian Automobile Factory in Turin had opened a large plant some ten years earlier. In 1903 FIAT started producing a truck that carried four tons of cargo. Highways were badly needed.

The road between Bologna and Florence linked the north to the rest of the country. Widening the old road was not worth the effort. There were too many sharp bends, the slopes were too steep. So they began to build a new one: the Strada Statale della Futa, so called after the name of a famous mountain pass. It was a huge project. The viaduct of Sant'Antonio, between Sabbioni and Loiano, looked like a Roman bridge.

One Saturday morning, Umberto took his son to see the viaduct in the horse-drawn carriage. He put the child on his shoulders and walked on it. Antonio was scared. He had never been in such a high place.

Umberto talked to the farmers who lived next door. He knew them a little because his wife owned a small farm not far away. Poor soil, steep fields. At home they called it the 'estate of hunger'.

"What a lovely child, Signor Ascari! Come in and have a glass of wine."

He entered the dark kitchen with his son. By the fire sat an old man. Umberto greeted him with respect. The man who had invited him put a bottle on the table. "Let's have a drink. I'll pour a drop also for your son. It's sparkling and sweet."

The farmer's wife arrived with a plate, and said to the child: "Here's a cake. And it's a good one."

Antonio did not know what to do. He looked at his father.

"Come on! That cake looks really good. And today we'll let you dip it into the wine."

The kitchen was black with smoke and Antonio was a little intimidated, but the lady with the apron smiled: "He looks exactly like his father!"

The child reached for the cake. The grains of sugar glittered like ice in the yard.

"What do you say?" asked Umberto. A dim "thank you" was heard. Antonio held his cake. They would not take it away from him.

4th January 1911, Loiano.

Outside it was cold and raining. His mother did not want him to go out that morning. Antonio was bored. He sat on the wicker loveseat by the window. His father saw him there all alone. "Well, what are you doing? Are you bored? Come here."

Antonio's father took him by his hand. He made a funny face and put a finger to his mouth, "Shush... Let's go and steal something from your mother."

Without speaking, he took him into the linen room. Lying on the table was a brown cloth that women used for ironing. His father tucked it under his jacket, pretending to hide it. "Now we have to steal the beans..."

There was nobody in the kitchen. Umberto opened the cupboard. He picked up the jar of beans and off they went to Antonio's room.

"Now stretch the cloth on the floor. Not like that: it must not be smooth. You have to make mountains. Pick up those books."

Antonio was beginning to have fun.

"That's it. Put the largest at the bottom and the little ones above, then cover them with a cloth and you already have a mountain. You can make mountains even with pillows. No, not the one you sleep on, otherwise your Mum will get angry. Steal a pillow from the ottoman sofa in the other room."

Valleys and hills took shape.

"Now we need soldiers. Italians against Austrians, as in the Wars of Independence, before I was born. Austrians were everywhere in Italy. They were wicked! Then the Savoia came from Piedmont to fight them."

Antonio listened attentively.

"White beans are the Italians, while the speckled ones, the beans with 'eyes', are the Austrians. When you find a red bean, then it's an officer. Italians are the Hunters of the Alps. This bean here, which is red and larger than the others, is Garibaldi."

A new world opened before the eyes of Antonio. The rain outside did not matter any more.

2nd November 1914, Loiano.

Benizia opened the shutters. The fog was so thick that the mountains in front of the house couldn't be seen. She didn't light the lamp, though. She knew how to dress in the dark.

When she was in the kitchen, daylight began to rise, but it had started to rain. As a child, bad weather had not saddened her, but as the years went by... If only she could be Veronica's age.

I'd better move. What is it I have to do?

It was All Souls, the day Benizia gave alms to the poor. She took two chairs and put them by the door. Then she took the two bags of flour – one white and one yellow – which Evangelista, the servant, had filled the day before. She put one on each chair. She took out a tin ladle. When the village poor arrived, she would give them a ladle or two, depending on their needs. She rubbed the flour between her fingers. She had liked its softness since her childhood, when her father owned the village bakery.

She fed the chickens and brought home three eggs. They were still warm. She would prepare eggnog for Veronica. She would make it white and creamy. Back in the kitchen, she heard a knock.

"I'm coming!" she exclaimed, hurrying towards the door.

She expected to see an old crone, wearing an apron and with a dark scarf around her head, but it was a blue-eyed child who smiled at her.

"Clara, come in. What a fog we have today!"

Now and then the girl brought water from the well to Benizia's home, and she in turn gave her a little coin or a sweetie.

"Come with me," she said, "let's wake up Veronica. I'll make eggnog for you both."

Soon after, Benizia came down the stairs with a child on each hand. Evangelista was in the kitchen. He had lit the fire but he was old and he had already dozed off next to the fire. Benizia sat the girls at the big table, with a blanket around their legs, and she began to tell them about the time when she was also a child and she ran in the meadows, even in winter...

27th June 1915, Loiano.

He was a father for the third time. Another boy. And to think that he was almost fifty! He was still sprightly, however, still a handsome man, Umberto thought that morning while shaving, careful not to spoil his moustache.

It was he who had decided on the name. Giulio, like Giulio Cesare, the Roman Emperor. The right name to be somebody.

The baptism would take place in two hours. Before going out, Umberto glanced at the big table which was already laid for the feast. From the kitchen came noises and voices. Better let the women work. He would certainly not be of any help.

He walked into the village with his stick and hat, pleased with himself and with life.

In the café on the square, however, they were all talking of the dead, even though it was only a month since Italy had declared war on Austria.

"And Michelini, poor fellow!" said a short man. "What a fate! He was born in '89. I saw his wife on the day of the funeral. She was as white as a sheet. She's still young, with two children! And they have no money. Poor woman!"

Umberto was not happy. That day, when he was celebrating the arrival of his third child, was for others a day of mourning. He decided to say nothing of the baptism. He soon returned home to get his wife.

The ceremony was long. Don Alfonso, who was getting old, could no longer see well. Sometimes he lost his place while reading the service, although he should have known it by heart.

Little Giulio at some point began to cry. Then he fell asleep. You could see it had done him good because when the priest poured water on his head he did not even put out a groan. He only opened his big eyes and looked at him. He was a bright boy. You could tell right away.

3rd October 1916, Strada.

"Oh, come on! You're not leaving for the war..." With these words Don Severo called out to Antonio and his cousin Francesco at Bologna station, when it was time to say goodbye. Antonio's face was streaked with tears. Aunt Teresa gave him a peck on the cheek. Part reproach, part caress. Then they got into the car.

His cousin Francesco was now thirteen and put on the air of a grown up, but Antonio was eleven and it seemed to him that the world was collapsing. They were leaving for Strada, a small town in the Casentino region, a faraway place. Antonio did not understand. Why could he not go to school closer to home?

He did not know that Aunt Teresa had insisted with his mother that he was sent to school with Francesco. Teresa had chosen Strada hoping that Don Severo, who was a family friend, would help her son behave, and maybe give him some encouragement. The truth was Francesco did not like to study, and his poor mother, who no longer had a husband, had to lean on someone.

To hearten the two boys before departure, Teresa had given each of them a fine book by Salgari: *The Tigers of Mompracem* to Antonio and *The Conquest of an Empire* to Francesco. While travelling by train, Antonio had permission to read aloud, so his cousin could hear. "*On the night of 20th December, 1849 a violent storm...*"

"Lower your voice," said Don Severo. "We don't want to disturb other people."

La canzone del Piave

5th November 1918, morning, Bologna.

"The Augsburg Empire is dissolved. The Alliance grants the armistice to the defeated army." Umberto read these words in a newspaper on that Tuesday morning, while sitting in a café.

What a memorable day! There was something festive in the air, a special kind of happiness. Everybody was walking lightly, without a care in the world.

The young woman at the counter had smiled at him as sweetly as never before. The man behind the bar was simply flying. He managed to be everywhere at once, elated to do his job, ready to serve each and everyone with invariable grace and a perfect flourish. A king serving kings. And each time, after taking an order or chatting amiably with a lady, he resumed singing a popular war song:

Il Piave mormorava calmo e placido al passaggio

dei primi fanti il ventiquattro maggio...

Those words had a special meaning that day. The war had begun on 24th May 1915. Over three years had elapsed and at last the conflict was over.

When Umberto heard the bells ring the day before, he had immediately understood. Yet it still seemed unreal. He could not believe his eyes even then, while reading those capital letters: "*PROCLAMATION OF VICTORY*".

After 41 months of uninterrupted and the harshest fighting, the Italian army, led by His Majesty the King, had won. The Proclamation ended with a sentence that Umberto read over and over again, each time feeling younger and stronger: *"The remains of what was one of the most powerful armies in the entire world are heading back north – disorderly and without hope – along the valleys they previously descended with proud confidence."*

5th November 1918, evening, Bologna.

Perhaps it was not the right day to go. There would certainly be a lot of people. And then with the Spanish flu that had been recently raging in Bologna... Yet, how could you not celebrate? The war was over! Umberto and his friends had dined at a good restaurant. They knew the cook and were always treated like princes.

When they left, it was too early to go to bed. They had been drinking. They were in high spirits. There were so many places where they could stop for another glass of wine. When one of them suggested, "Let's go to an *osteria*," another replied, with a suggestive tone, "And a certain number in Via dei Poeti?" Umberto had not been there for a long time, but he was still young, after all, and that night he felt like a lion. And then his wife...

"Let's line up in pairs!" said he.

They walked towards the alley. Wine warmed them up. Here was the house on the right. The door opened thanks to a knob that you pulled from outside. No need to ring the bell and wait in the street.

The hall was feebly lit by a lamp. From the first floor voices and laughter could be heard. Somebody was singing. A double row of rooms opened on a long corridor. The first to the left was a waiting room. There was a piano and a dresser which was surmounted by a mirror. On the marble top an assortment of liqueur glasses and half-empty bottles lay scattered.

"Is Magda there?" Umberto asked the maîtresse.

"If you would be so kind to wait five minutes. A toast to our country, gentlemen?"

Umberto, however, no longer felt like drinking. He sat in a corner with a listless air. He started thinking of his wife, his children. They did not give him much gratification. Did they really love him? Would they really miss him? In the end a man finds himself alone...

Magda was free. He was told this by a girl he had never seen before, a pretty girl, wearing a purple dressing gown, her make-up slightly faded. "Third door on the right." He already knew.

He entered the small square room. It felt warm in there.

"We haven't seen you for a while," said the woman.

"Tonight I wanted to celebrate."

Magda was filing a nail, sitting on a smooth bed. The linen had just been changed. She seemed to have worked enough for that night. Umberto let himself down next to her, fully dressed as he was. He stroked his forehead with both hands, to forestall the headache that he felt approaching.

"You're tired," she said.

He did not answer.

In her light blue satin dressing gown, the colour of the sky in the early morning, Magda lay down next to him, her head resting on his arm. With a finger she followed his profile, from the top of his forehead down to his neck, slowly, conveying through that gesture all the calm that her tiredness and the fatigue she sensed in him demanded. Then she started unbuttoning his shirt.

14th November 1919, Loiano.

Giulio, who was four years old, was a little bored in those autumn days because it soon became dark. His sister and brother were at the boarding school. His father was often in Bologna. He lived alone in that big house with his mother. He could not read yet. He was a child. Maria had told him all the tales she knew. The two house cats had grown old and crotchety. Once Giulio had tried to pull the grey cat's tail, just to make friends, and as a thank you he had received a scratch on his face. Since then he kept away.

That afternoon he was playing with his toy blocks: small blocks of wood in the shape of cubes, cylinders, pyramids, arches. Giulio was building a bridge. He was kneeling before the ottoman sofa, with his bare knees on the carpet, which pinched a little, and he had begun to put the blocks on top of each other. The ottoman mattress, however, was all bumpy, and the bricks wouldn't stand up. He had managed to make a beautiful building when, getting over-enthusiastic, he leaned his elbow on the mattress and plop: the bridge was all on the ground.

A wooden block had ended up under the ottoman, where he could not reach it. His mother was out at that moment. The only person in the house was Minghina, the cook. He went to ask her for help.

Minghina dropped to her knees and grabbed the toy. It was the block that went on top of the bell tower. The one Giulio liked most after the arch, but it had an even greater value because there was only one in the whole box.

Giulio smiled.

Minghina, seeing the child alone in that room, which was dimly lit and cold, said: "Come with me into the kitchen. I'll make something that you've never tasted. I bet you'll like it."

She lifted Giulio and sat him at the table. Even Minghina felt alone. Outside everything was black.

"Do you know what *miazzole* are?"

Giulio shook his head.

"You're old enough. You'll see... "

She picked up an aluminium pan. She poured a little flour into it. She added salt and a tablespoon of oil, then a little water, and she began to stir until, in Giulio's eyes, the flour had become like mud did when he played with it.

Giulio watched open-mouthed.

Minghina cut off a piece of lard, melted it in a blackened pan, then she said: "You're sitting there, eh! Remember that hot grease splashes and burns. Look here."

She took a spoonful of the whitish sauce and poured it in the hot melted lard. It sizzled up. Giulio liked the sound. And that strange smell. Years later, in distant lands, it would be the smell of home.

"Here are the *miazzole*, Signorino," said Minghina, presenting Giulio with a plate of deep-fried golden crumpets.

"Be careful, they're hot! I'll teach you how to eat them..." She cut a large slice of cheese. "A bit of cheese and a bit of *miazzola*."

Giulio, who was cautious, kept blowing the *miazzola* for a long time. Then he bit into it with some mistrust. It did not burn any more. It was crunchy on the outside and soft inside. It was salty and it tasted fried. It was the best thing he had ever eaten.

Youth

14th February 1923, Loiano.

Antonio knocked at his friend Lucio's door. They were going to watch a competition at the shooting hall in Valsicura.

"Come with me," said Lucio, but instead of going out he took him to his elder brother's room. He opened a drawer in the dresser and showed him a black shirt.

"My brother is joining the fascist militia," he said. "If I wanted, I could get into it too. You know you just have to be seventeen?"

Antonio said no, and his friend went on: "You know how the militia works? It's made up of legions, which are divided into cohorts, which are divided into centuriae, maniples and squads. Like the Roman legions."

After laying the shirt on the dresser, Lucio pulled a fez out of the drawer, laid it carefully on his head and made the Roman salute, looking into the mirror. "You can join us too, comrade!"

Antonio looked at Lucio's reflection in the mirror. Dressed like that he almost did not recognise him.

18th July 1923, Le Croci di Monzuno.

Every year Aunt Teresa went to Le Croci at the time of wheat threshing, to take a look at what was going on up there. And then at Le Croci it was cool in summer. It was heaven!

That year, Teresa had bought her son a car. She could afford it, and she would do anything for her son. Francesco on the other hand knew how to convince his mother.

Having a new car was great, but showing it around was even better. Thus, that morning Francesco had accompanied his mother to Loiano, where he strutted along the streets. Then he loaded his cousins Antonio and Veronica into the car and drove them on a trip up to Trasasso. He was the number one. The others were spectators! It was he who really *lived.*

"You know, Veronica," said Aunt Teresa, "at Le Croci there are two families of farmers. They are so hospitable that each day we have lunch with one family and dinner with the other. Otherwise they get offended. You'll see what a welcome we get! And the cheese..."

At Trasasso the road ended, but a farm wagon was waiting for them. To transport Signora Teresa in proper style, the team of oxen had been decorated with bows, while the bottom of the vehicle had been covered with striped mattresses and pillows. After rocking for nearly an hour on a continuously uphill trail, between straggling oaks, twisted hawthorns and no less prickly juniper shrubs, Teresa and her family arrived at Le Croci.

Two families worked the farm. About fifty people in all. More than twenty children.

When they reached the mountain ridge, they saw Loiano in the distance, on the other side of the valley. Antonio stopped to look at the thin row of houses, lit by the afternoon sun. He could make out the bell tower.

"The air's nice here, eh?" said Francesco. "Actually, you know what they say when it's windy? That the beautiful Venus is passing... No wonder, given the fact that we are close to Monte Venere, where she lives. I would be willing to encounter the beautiful Venus, but it seems she doesn't like me."

Antonio laughed. His cousin always made him laugh.

"The next time I'll come with my motorbike," said Francesco, pointing to a gravel road. "You'll see what a cloud of dust! I wonder if they have ever seen a motorbike up here."

Meanwhile Veronica helped her aunt unpack. They slept in the same room.

At dinner, Teresa, her son and her nephews entered the large square house next door. Melchiade, one of the farmers, greeted Signora Teresa saying: "Come in. It's your home!"

The whole family was standing next to a long table which was fully laid for the occasion.

Melchiade invited his guests to take their place. Antonio hesitated because there were few chairs. Then he discovered that only the head of the family and his eldest sons sat at the table. The women served, and the children went out to play.

Veronica did not know what to talk about with those big burly men, so she listened to Francesco and Antonio who discussed pheasant and partridge hunting, and the winter season. Sometimes it was so cold – Melchiade said – that the fountains froze. To drink, they melted snow on the stove.

After dinner, Evaristo pulled out the accordion and they all went to dance in the farmyard. Veronica had a ball, then she thought it best to sit next to her aunt. She asked an old lady to tell some ghost stories, and during the night she woke up at every noise.

She decided that Le Croci was a nice place, but she was a little afraid of it, starting from its name. Where there were crosses there were often tombs... And then Melchiade's neck was horribly inflated on one side. Her aunt told her he had a goitre. She had never seen a man with a goitre before.

2nd March 1924, Loiano.

Beep beep! When Maria heard the horn sound she knew it was Francesco. She heard the friction of the wheels curving into the gravel courtyard. She walked over to the window. She saw her nephew and his three friends getting out of his car with their load of dead thrushes.

Those boys all have little desire to work, thought Maria. She knew that Francesco could afford to live as a landowner. When they had nothing to do, however, men were up to no good. Her husband was a good example. And Francesco promised well! He was now twenty-one and had never done a day's work in his life. But he was very good at hunting. And he was good at spending money on cars and even on motorbikes!

Maria thought of her sister. Poor Teresa. She had spoiled him and now it was too late. She had never told her in so many words, but it was apparent she was not happy.

Maria heard Francesco and his friends' voices in the yard. Francesco was addressing Maria's cook, Minghina. "I'll do everything myself, Minghina! Don't you know I'm good at cooking? Then when the thrushes are ready I'll invite you to dinner. So for once you will just sit down and be a lady, instead of standing at the stove."

What kind of talk is that? Maria thought: *and where do you want a cook to be?* Having lost patience with her nephew, she returned to what she was doing. She was mending Giulio's trousers.

Francesco opened the shutters, as the house smelled fuggy since it was seldom visited: the part of the house that had fallen to Teresa after her mother's death.

Meanwhile, Antonio came up from the village. He saw the open shutters and realised that his cousin was there. He liked Francesco, who was bigger than him and who looked defiant. When he knocked on the door, it was his cousin who opened it. "You've come at the right time. Give me a hand to light the fire if you don't want the whole house to burn down!"

While Antonio was taking care of the wood, Francesco opened a bottle, and his friends began to drink. "Oh, you know what happened to my uncle?" – said one – "He started quarrelling with his wife on the horse-drawn trap, in the countryside on their way home. He was so engrossed that he let go of the reins and the horse went on alone. They were arguing and arguing until the horse stopped... at the door of the brothel. He says that since that day she's never talked to him again!"

Everyone laughed. The fire crackled. It was time to think about the thrushes.

"Oh, but isn't it necessary to let them hang until they get high?"

"They should be good already."

They put the thrushes on a spit, but when one of Francesco's friends bit into the little bird, he spat it on the plate: "Nice joke! They are disgustingly sweet, you idiot!"

"I can't believe it: I mixed up the salt with the sugar," Francesco said, clapping his hands. He started laughing: "I don't know the kitchen. I'm not the cook round here!"

"It's your head that needs salting," said another friend as he opened the cans to check.

There was only one thing to do, and it was Antonio who suggested it: "Let's ask Minghina what she can do."

Minghina brought them two fine capons. They dined on those, and repeatedly drank to her health. When Maria closed her shutters, they were still laughing. Luckily Francesco did not often come to Loiano. Otherwise he would have spoiled her son.

9th May 1925, Loiano.

For the first time Antonio was in love. That Saturday he had gone on a trip with Veronica and their friends. Giulio had also wanted to be part of the group. They had allowed him to carry the food basket, for they had planned to breakfast in the meadows. It was Veronica who had thought of an English picnic.

At one point, Elsa had asked him to accompany her to a nearby spring. When it was time to drink he helped her, and when she raised her face, her lips still wet with water, he approached her and gave her a kiss. Elsa did not say anything.

As they walked back, she only added: "You know I've never kissed a boy." Antonio felt proud. He had been the first. She had not pulled back. Then he was not so bad, if such a beautiful girl liked him.

That day they did not have any other opportunity to be alone. He had the impression that Elsa was avoiding him. It was up to him to be accepted by her. It is always the man who courts.

The next day and the next he could think of nothing else but Elsa. He walked down to the village over and over again, yet there was no sign of her. Was she angry because of what had happened? He had to be sure. He had to tell her how much he loved her. But how?

A letter! Only, he was not good at writing. Had he been asked to recount the deeds of Yanez and his Tigers in Salgari's novels that would have been easy, but what did a girl want to hear?

To write that letter another girl was needed. He thought of Veronica. She would not let him down.

"Fine. I will write the letter," Veronica said: "but it's three cigarettes a page."

Antonio was stunned. Then he laughed. "Deal."

26th September 1925, Loiano.

"What shall we do about this boy?" Maria asked, turning to her husband. They did not talk much, she and Umberto, but when it came to the children they had to take decisions. "He's twenty, you know. He's a man! Now that he goes out with Elsa... he won't be able to marry without a job!"

Even Umberto had thought of this. His son was a man, but he did not have a clear path ahead. He had studied for a while. Then at some point they had taken him out of boarding school. Not only was he not particularly keen, but boarding school was expensive! Result: Antonio had not learnt anything useful. Of course he had nice ways. He was a good boy.

"Listen to me, Maria. I know what to do. Let's renovate the farmhouse and open a hotel. It *is* a beautiful house, still new. The location is right, fronting the street. Where the stable is we'll have the dining room. In the barn there's space for six rooms. It won't take too much money. I'll explain to him how to run a hotel. Antonio won't take long to learn."

"Everything looks easy to you, but it's me who has to find the money," was Maria's answer.

"I'll take care of the furniture, but what really matters is finding the right name. You told me that where the farm house now stands there used to be an inn for pilgrims. Let's call it *Albergo Pellegrino.* What do you think? Would you stop at the Albergo Pellegrino? Of course the food will have to be gorgeous!"

31st October 1926, Bologna.

Mussolini was inaugurating the Stadio Littoriale. The founding stone had been set in June 1925 by no less than His

Majesty King Vittorio Emanuele III. It was Leandro Arpinati, the fascist Mayor of Bologna, who had launched the project.

On that October morning the Duce – as Mussolini was called – had entered the stadium on horseback. The weather was fine. The ceremony had been a success.

In the city centre, the streets were packed with people. Some held little flags in their hands. Others wore their black shirts or the medals they had obtained during the war. They all wanted to see the Duce, to be there on that day.

Umberto was sitting in a café in Piazza Maggiore. He pretended not to care, but he was curious to see the great man. When he realised that the time was approaching, he walked towards Via Rizzoli.

Mussolini's car was driving along the street. From the neighbouring houses flowers were falling to the ground.

Suddenly, a youth sneaked between the soldiers and aimed at Mussolini with a pistol. Before people realised what was happening, a Marshal of the *Carabinieri* Corps threw himself against the youth to deflect the shot. Mussolini was unscathed.

The youth was lynched by Arpinati's men. His name was Anteo Zamboni. He was fifteen.

Umberto had seen nothing because the crowd in front of him was too thick, but that shot and the following shouts were engraved in his memory. He met a friend who was no less shaken, and they sat down with a glass of wine. It was time to meditate.

26th March 1927, Loiano.

It was not yet eleven and the bend at the Albergo Pellegrino already overflowed with spectators. The only talk was of the Mille Miglia. A thousand mile race!

"The first car to start is Maggi and Maserati's Isotta Fraschini."

"What's the route?"

"A thousand miles is one thousand, six hundred kilometres."

"I thought it would be fewer."

"They left Brescia at eight. There are seventy-seven cars!"

"My dear fellow, it's the race of the century!"

"And after Loiano, where do they go?"

"From Florence they go to Siena, Viterbo and Rome. Back up through Perugia and Ancona, on to Bologna. Then they go to Padua and finally arrive at Brescia. It's in the shape of an eight."

There were those who had brought bread and salami, and even a bottle of wine. Alongside men, wearing caps or hats, the uniformed *Carabinieri* were engrossed in their role as 'guarantors of security'. Antonio opened up a first-floor room to the ladies so that they could watch the race from above.

Suddenly they heard a distant rumble. At one moment it was far off, at a sharp bend, and the next it was approaching.

The rumble became a roar.

Everybody was standing, shouting, their arms raised. The joy, the speed, the life!

Broom, broom. Gearing down, then gaining speed again. A cloud of smoke.

"It's number 42. Brilli Peri and Pesenti's Alfa Romeo."

A deafening noise was heard. Somebody cried: "Here are the other cars!"

Antonio recognised number 89: Nuvolari and Cappelli's Bianchi.

Someone shouted: "Here's 49. The driver calls himself 'Brother unknown'."

Antonio looked at his little brother: "You'd like to drive a car like that, eh!"

Giulio looked up at him. His eyes were full of joy.

29th June 1927, Loiano.

"Come on, Roberto, let's stop here to have a bite. I cannot put up with these bends any longer!"

"Ah, but I wanted to have lunch in Tuscany, Mummy."

"Look, Rossana, your mother is right. I'm hungry too."

So it was that the car with a Novara licence plate stopped at the Albergo Pellegrino. Rossana and her friend Pina had attended the conservatory together. As a gift for graduation, Rossana's parents were driving them to Florence to hear a famous pianist.

"What a beautiful dining room, with arches!" Rossana did not know that this had been a stable.

"We are eating outside," said mother, who suffered from hot flushes. "There's a nice terrace. And I like climbing roses."

The restaurant was good and after lunch they asked to see the rooms. Everything was clean and tidy. "How young the owner is," said Rossana as they got into the car. "Cute too!"

Pina did not comment, but when they were driving back from Florence and it was time to decide where to spend the night, she ventured: "What if instead of going to Bologna, we stopped in Loiano? Such a nice little village."

30th September 1927, Loiano.

It could not go on like this. He had to clarify things and get it over with. For the past three months Pina and he had been exchanging love letters, and this time it was not Veronica who wrote them... Moreover, a couple of times he had taken a train to Novara, on the sly. He had told his family that he needed to stop in Bologna because of the hotel, and he had run away.

Elsa saw that he had changed. He could not make a fool of her. She did not deserve it. She was a good girl, and he was a scoundrel.

He was ready to give up everything. To start a new life. Pina had given him courage. She said that her father was the director of a textile factory. She would help him find a job in Novara, if he really wanted to marry her.

Antonio had always dreamed of getting away. He saw people driving past Loiano all day long, headed God knows where, but he... where was *he* going?

He talked to his father. The only one who could understand. Antonio knew that they had opened the hotel for him, but he did not feel right about this. Then he would speak with Elsa. The thought made him shudder.

21st June 1928, Novara.

Pina and Antonio were holding each other in bed. Pina had put on a record. Toscanini conducting *La Bohème*. Mimì sang her desperate craving for life:

Ma quando vien lo sgelo
il primo sole è mio,
il primo bacio dell'aprile è mio...

Passion was born. Music enveloped Mimì and Rodolfo, enveloped Pina and Antonio. Soon after, with the word love, the act was over. The record continued to spin. Neither of them got up.

"To think that so many years went by before you and I knew each other. I wonder what you were doing on a certain day... On 21st June 1921! The first day of summer, like today, and I didn't even know you existed. And you didn't know I existed."

"Our lives were running their course" – Pina said – "and we didn't know that one day we would meet. It's beautiful. And also sad because who knows how many people never meet!"

Antonio smiled: "Perhaps, if two persons are destined to meet, then they will really meet." He was happy that the threads of their lives had knotted. He kissed her on the neck. He felt a desire that was reciprocated. After making love again they remained motionless, while they cooled down.

"I've thought it over, you know, but I just cannot remember where I was on that 21st June. I was sixteen. I was probably wasting time. I'm certain I didn't do anything important."

"Everything you've done is important to me. Because you're you."

Antonio did not even look at her. He searched for her fingers and they remained immersed in silence.

28th November 1929, Loiano.

The shame! The shame! Umberto could not get any sleep. He had occupied a separate room for years. It had been his wife's choice. At first it had not annoyed him too much. She was not the only woman in the world... That night, however, he hated her. That night he felt exiled, chased from the place that was rightfully his, treated as a half-wit in his own house. The idea of going away, far from it all, crossed his mind. But where? The shame! She was a witch!

Umberto thought of his children, of the bunch of promissory notes in the dresser drawer. He thought of the farm near Monghidoro that he had sold because of gambling debts. He thought of the money he had inherited from his brother Ferruccio, who had died while waiting to emigrate to Asmara, in Eritrea. He thought of the nights he had spent gambling, in Bologna, in Loiano.

And what was wrong with that? After all he had never beaten her. It would have done her good!

She had refused to sign. She had refused him her money. *You won't get anything from me! Nothing at all!* The words hammered in his head. He was not old. He was sixty-three. He only wanted to die.

8th February 1930, Loiano.

He felt so tired. His throat was aching. His head was spinning. He lost the thread of his thoughts. That funeral had done him no good. He had come back the day before from Novara. Pina's father had died, and he had really felt somebody should be present at the funeral. He had caught cold. That was all he needed! He was fed up with living and fighting. His children had grown up. His wife... Well, they did not have much in common.

When Veronica came into his room to inquire about his health, he answered: "Call Doctor Visani."

After visiting him, the physician ordered: "*Letto, latte, lana!*" – Bed, milk and wool! – "You've got it this time. Beware not to catch pneumonia. Do nothing until my next visit. You're under house arrest!"

Visani went to see him every night, but Umberto was more and more tired. One night Visani stopped to talk with Maria, in a room on the other side of the house. In a soft tone, he advised that she had better call the priest. Her husband would not last long.

Umberto had always thought of death as something that concerned others. This time, however, it was different. He felt so exhausted. As if he had no longer the strength to cling on. Letting go was sweet. It was living that proved tiring.

When he heard the voices in the corridor, and he saw the door opening, and Maria let the priest into the room, Umberto recovered his strength. What did they take him for? Did they think that he would leave like that? He discovered he was afraid of death, so afraid that he could harbour no other thought.

He had never seen death in the face until then. She had the face of that man dressed in black who was approaching him with his yellow teeth and his unctuous smile.

So it was all over. Like that? With no time to get used to the idea?

It was time to go. But *where?* He knew of no other places except for life.

These thoughts crossed his mind with the speed of lightning, and when the priest approached his bed, with his purple stole and the holy water, he understood.

He did not want to die, and with an uncontrollable repugnance for the man announcing his death, he hid his face under the cover. The priest interpreted his gesture as a refusal and left the room in silence. Besides, he had never seen Umberto in church.

Flying Away

14th May 1931, Bologna.

Since 1922 every public performance of the Royal March had been followed by a rendition of *Giovinezza* – Youth, the Hymn of the National Fascist Party. And when important personages were present at the theatre the performance was preceded by both anthems. That evening Maestro Arturo Toscanini was to conduct at the *Teatro Comunale* to commemorate the composer Giuseppe Martucci, who had been his friend. For ten days he had been in Bologna for rehearsal. He wanted everything to be perfect.

Only the day before the concert the rumour leaked out that Costanzo Ciano, Minister of Communications and father of Mussolini's son-in-law, would be present at the theatre. He would be accompanied by Leandro Arpinati, Under-Secretary for the Interior and former *Podestà* – the fascist Mayor – of Bologna. The two politicians were in Bologna to inaugurate the cable car that led to the shrine of San Luca, a beacon of progress. Each cabin could carry as many as eighteen passengers.

Toscanini, however, refused to open the evening with the two anthems. He thought that the lively music would mar the commemoration. A different ambience was required. He told his musicians: "Gentlemen, be democrats in life and aristocrats in art!" Less than a month earlier Toscanini had refused to perform *Giovinezza* at the opening of *Turandot* at *La Scala*, and Mussolini had stayed at home to avoid confrontation.

At five in the afternoon a compromise was reached: when Ciano and Arpinati entered, a band would play the Royal March and *Giovinezza* in the foyer. Toscanini's refusal, however, was still making the fascists fume. At eight, the organisers informed him that he was expected to conduct the anthems.

Change of plans around nine, when the concert approached: "Maestro, you must excuse me if I disturb you again, but you understand the difficulties of the moment. I have good news, though. The Minister and the Under-Secretary are dining at a restaurant. They won't be at the *Teatro Comunale*, that's for sure. For the concert there are no obstacles."

"Finally they've got it," said Toscanini to his wife, after putting down the phone. "And now let's think of poor Martucci, who did not deserve this farce."

The trap had been set.

In fascist circles tension was high. The news of the confrontation with Toscanini had got round the city, and discontent grew.

When the Maestro's car reached the side entrance of the theatre, a group of young fascists was waiting there. Toscanini, who was not afraid of anyone, came out, but he was welcomed with whistles and bad words. He did not expect, however, that they would pass from pushing to punching.

"What are you doing? Stop! This is Toscanini," cried his driver as he tried to protect him, but the Maestro took a blow on the head while a slap cut his lip.

The theatre ushers intervened. He was escorted away from the crowd and back to his hotel, in front of which the fascists soon gathered.

Toscanini and his wife Carla were in their room, discussing what to do, when they heard knocking. It was Ottorino Respighi, the composer, who was born in Bologna and knew the city. For fifteen years Toscanini had taken his works all over the world. The two were friends.

Respighi had a sickly look, like somebody attending a funeral: "You have to leave Bologna by six in the morning. Otherwise they will not answer for your safety."

Carla began to cry. "What's going on?"

Toscanini did not hesitate for an instant. He turned to the driver: "Get the car ready. I will not stay here an hour longer. Mine is not an escape. They are the ones who will regret it!"

The Maestro had left from the side of the building, but the fascists continued to surround the main entrance of the hotel, chanting and shouting, until the owner came out: "Look, Toscanini is already far from Bologna. And my clients cannot sleep. Take this" – he said, giving them money: "Go drink to my health."

They went away singing:

All'armi! All'armi siam fascisti,
terror dei comunisti...

Some went to a tavern, some went to a brothel.

15th May 1931, Bologna.

When Antonio woke up, his thoughts wandered back to the night before. Pina had always dreamed of listening to Toscanini conducting in a theatre. In the past, they had decided to go to hear him at La Scala. From Novara to Milan the trip was short. But in the end they had not been able to. So when Pina had heard about the concert in Bologna, Antonio had phoned an old friend.

Although they had not seen each other for years he had been very kind and had bought him the tickets.

Pina and Antonio arrived in Bologna in the afternoon, just in time to visit the hotel, wash, change their clothes, get something to eat and run to the theatre.

Things, however, did not turn out right. They were kept there in the hall waiting and waiting. At one point the audience began to clap. It really was time to start! Then the news spread. The concert was cancelled. No one knew why.

Once outside, they realised that something was wrong. A group of fascists was singing their hearts out. There was tension in the air.

A gentleman was speaking, surrounded by a crowd of faces: "I tell you that Toscanini has been given his due! They taught him a lesson."

A woman next to Antonio turned her head towards a man: "Who are they? What's he talking about?"

"The fascists," the man answered in a low tone.

The woman opened her mouth as if to make an exclamation.

Antonio could not understand, but he was struck by an absolute certainty. He would never hear Toscanini conducting.

11th January 1932, Lunatic Asylum, Imola, Province of Bologna.

Why had he been locked up in that room? Why had they taken his clothes? Francesco was there, wearing those strange striped pyjamas. He got up from bed and approached the door. There was no handle. He tried pushing it hard with his shoulder. Nothing happened. His arm ached.

In the middle of the door was a peephole. To see out into the corridor, you had to squeeze your nose against the slit. The white paint was badly peeling. He wondered why he had been locked in there. What place was this? He began to call "help help help help."

He heard footsteps in the corridor. The door opened. They had heard him. They were coming to rescue him. Instead it was a backhanded slap. "You shut up! What are you screaming for?"

No one had ever treated him like that. Where had he ended up? He resumed screaming "help help help." The door before him was open. A head butt in the belly caused the male nurse to double over. The corridor. Freedom.

Francesco ran, ran, ran towards the staircase. How did he know where the staircase was? It did not matter. The race seemed endless. The corridor was shiny and slippery. Around the corner they were on him.

Why were they shouting? Why did they want to keep him in that place? They took him to a room. They took his pyjamas. They wrapped him in a gown that was open at the back. They tied him to a wooden bed that had no mattress. There was a hole in the middle of the planks. The room stank.

"Now you stay there! If you need to shit or piss, you'll just have to do it. See you tomorrow!"

Francesco pulled with all his might, as if everything, everything depended on it. He had to escape, he had to go, he had to return home. He started crying, thinking of the evil witch who had stolen his life. What had happened?

"Mum," he found himself moaning. "Where are you? Mum!"

19th February 1932, Imola.

Antonio could not believe that his cousin had ended up like that. Rumours had come through Veronica that strange things had happened, but this... A madhouse! They had not been able to keep him at home, Veronica had told him on the phone.

He did not have the courage to write to Aunt Teresa, but he could not leave Francesco alone, although he had not seen him in years. And to think that Bologna and Novara were not far away. Why had he not turned up before? Not even when he returned to Bologna to hear Toscanini. Why had he broken all ties with his former life?

He had asked for a day off. He had woken up early and he had taken a train from Novara to Imola. It was the saddest of trips. Outside there was a thick fog, as if that morning the sun did not want to rise.

He thought back to when he and Francesco had gone to boarding school. Leaving home. Abandoning everything. Yet, in boarding school they had grown up year after year. And they had gone back home every Christmas, every Easter, every summer.

Life was like that. You formed habits, a sheltering cocoon. Then you were forced to say goodbye to it all. But each end was also a beginning. You entered a new stage, you started to form new habits. There was hope, something to look forward to.

Yet, no one came out of the asylum. That was the end of Francesco, not even the end, a limbo, just waiting and waiting for time to pass, for time to kill itself. He could not even think of it. How could he help his cousin?

According to Veronica it was because of a metal filling in a tooth. It had caused an infection. Could it be true?

Before travelling to Imola, he had made a phone call. He did not want to risk not seeing Francesco. He had to lay a hand on his shoulder. He had to tell him that he loved him.

Suddenly he felt his eyes swell. He clenched his teeth. From the train window, he looked at the flat plain, at the scattered houses, with their chimneys smoking. Families that would meet that evening. Lives that went on as ever.

When he got to the station, he entered a café and asked for a *grappa*. At each step, his feet seemed heavier. He wondered if he should turn back and go home. Yet he went on and on, repeatedly asking for directions and yet getting lost, as if the town had turned into a labyrinth.

The asylum was housed in an ancient fortress. When Antonio approached its squat circular towers, the thought of Francesco, who was on the other side of those walls, became almost unbearable. He had to do something, to speak to him, to set him free.

He found the strength to ring the bell.

An attendant opened the door. He talked to a doctor. In principle, they would let him in, but one had to see how the patient was that day. The doctor led the way into the room, then he went out and made a sign to him to go in.

Antonio wanted to smile, but he couldn't. He did not even know who he was. He took two steps into that cell, without seeing anything.

Francesco was in front of him, his head shaven.

When Antonio approached, Francesco remained silent, his hands resting on the headboard of the bed, as if he was thinking. Then he in turn walked towards him.

"I hate you I hate you I hate you I hate you," he said, beating his fists on his own chest. From his look of a wounded beast, Antonio knew he had recognised him, but could not reach him. The doctor came. He put Francesco back in his place with a few words.

"It depends on the day," he said. "Try coming again."

Before leaving, Antonio gave Francesco a last look, but his cousin held his head turned to the wall, as if in shame.

Antonio did not have the courage to take the train to Imola again.

17th July 1933, Novara.

While walking on the street that morning, Antonio was daydreaming. He was on board an *SIAI Marchetti* seaplane, part of Italo Balbo's squadron, the most famous aviator of their time. He was taking part in a historic feat – the transatlantic flight from Rome to Chicago. Around him and the co-pilot only thousands of miles of water.

Here was the coast of Labrador! He saw himself getting off the plane, being carried in triumph by the crowd, along with the other *Trasvolatori*. They were heroes!

He suddenly came back down to earth. He felt slightly giddy.

For years Novara had been his city. He had no nostalgia for the Apennines. He liked the large Po valley, with its stately waterway heading to the sea, with its network of roads which led everywhere. He felt free there.

He travelled with his head rather than his body, but he was happy about his life. What had to happen to him had already happened. Leaving behind Elsa and his home village. Starting a new life.

When he made a trip to the countryside with Pina, he enjoyed watching the sky reflected in the rice fields. Green blades emerged from the clouds. Then a frog took a jump, causing concentric circles to flow, the sky to ripple. Finally all was calm again.

Life was like that: long periods when the water was smooth, all of a sudden a jump, a ripple of waves, then calm was restored. He wondered if he was bored, but he liked the regular rhythm of his days.

He liked walking to the cotton mill in the morning. It was the best time of the day. Everything was new and that moment was just for him. The city was waking up. The bicycles. Just a few trucks. That morning hour had a strange poetry.

Antonio walked along a stretch of canal. He listened to the voices and silences. He enjoyed trifling things. Once he arrived at work, he put on his overall.

In the evening his wife was waiting for him at home. That evening, perhaps, they would eat an ice cream in the square next to the Duomo. There was sweetness in that smooth-running life. What was the point of asking for more, he thought, when you are already happy?

15th October 1937, Bologna.

Poor Teresa, what a life you had! So thought Teresa on that October day, sitting in her home in Via Castiglione. She lost her husband when she was not yet thirty. Then it was the turn of her son Francesco. Locked in a mental hospital. A handsome and healthy and clever boy. And now here she was: a widow, with no children, almost blind.

The only person left was Antenesca, who had been with her since she was a child. She heard the doorbell, then the steps of Antenesca, who opened the door, and the voice of a man. Reaching towards a shadow, Teresa greeted the friar who had come to comfort her. "Would you like some coffee?"

"A drop if it's not too much trouble."

She heard Antenesca bustle. She heard everything. She knew everything. She was interested in nothing.

"How are you?" asked the friar.

"As God wills."

"The will of God is inscrutable. We must bow to His Providence. Sometimes God strikes those he loves most."

"It must mean that He loves me quite a lot," said Teresa, a little resentfully.

"We must not blaspheme. We must never be ungrateful. For even when God seems to take away everything from us, the gifts He has given us are still so many, first of all the gift of faith."

"Here's your coffee, Father," said Antenesca entering the room.

"Sugar?"

"Only two, thank you!"

"Would you like a *dolce*? I made them yesterday."

"If you insist."

"I'm tempted to speak clearly," said the friar, after gulping down the coffee and a couple of biscuits.

"Feel free to speak. My ears are still good," said Teresa, who often grew irritated during the friar's visits.

"Sometimes if God continues to strike at us it is to send us a message. It is for us to understand what it means!"

"I must be hard of understanding!" Teresa snapped.

"I've been thinking about your case. I pondered and prayed, and there's one thing I must tell you in good conscience."

Teresa kept silent.

"There is no doubt that your family is marked. One might almost say that God had a special reason to strike you, as if to force your hand, or more likely to give you an opportunity to change your behaviour. You who are so good, so pious. Why – I wondered – would God ever be displeased with you? And then I understood. Your home, where you have been kind enough to invite me on the Feast of the Pardon of Assisi. Well, you know that San Benedetto was a convent, a place consecrated to God, and what is once consecrated to God is consecrated forever, as in the bond of marriage!"

Teresa listened attentively, not a single muscle moving.

"That convent was alienated from Holy Mother Church, to which it belonged, by the disbelievers who made our country what it is, but in the eyes of God it is still sacred. In short, the best way to remedy the outrage that has been committed, thus driving away the curse that weighs on your family," – here he raised his hand to Heaven, forgetting that she could not see – "is to return to the Church what rightfully belongs to it."

Teresa went white. She was shivering and trembling, she did not know whether with fear or anger. She told the monk that she had grown tired. She called Antenesca and asked her to accompany the friar to the door.

When Antenesca returned, she told her: "If he comes back, tell him I'm out. If he comes back again, tell him that he's not welcome."

2nd April 1938, Bologna.

A man walked into a café. He looked shaken. He ordered a cognac. He did not wait for them to ask him. He could no longer keep to himself what he had seen.

"Have you heard what's happened?"

Behind the counter, the bartender raised his hands and his eyebrows. He had no idea, but he realised that there was talk of trouble.

"I'd gone to see the Mille Miglia on the avenues. It was full of people. Everyone was happy. A celebration! In short, number 101, a Lancia Aprilia, arrives, when – not far from where I was standing, perhaps ten feet away – it skids. It plunges into the crowd... "

The man put his hand to his forehead. He began to tremble. The bartender was speechless. The customers too.

"There were children, adults. I don't know how many have been taken away. I don't even know who is dead and who is wounded. All those people were there to have fun! All that blood on the pavement."

His head was spinning and he leaned his elbows on the counter.

The bartender's hand rested on his shoulder.

"No one understood why. Perhaps the tramlines? Perhaps a wheel that slipped... What it was I do not know!" He wiped his face with his hand, his back to the people who had gathered round him. "How much is the cognac?"

"Nothing."

Two customers rushed out of the café. They wanted to see what had happened. One of them bumped into an old lady, who was entering the café, leaning on a young woman. In his haste he did not apologize. "That's very rude," said Teresa.

The echo of the disaster was huge. The government decided that the Mille Miglia would no longer run on national roads.

War

10th June 1940, Travesio, in the Friuli region,
north-east of Venice.

In the café the silence was deep. They were all next to the radio. Mussolini was speaking from the balcony of Palazzo Venezia, in Rome.

Fighters of land, sea and air! Blackshirts of the revolution and of the legions! Men and women of Italy, of the Empire and the kingdom of Albania! Listen! The hour marked by fate is sounding in the sky of our homeland. The hour of irrevocable decisions. The declaration of war has already been delivered to the ambassadors of Great Britain and France.

Amalia did not say a word. She continued to dry the glasses behind the bar. She thought of the mothers who had seen their children die. She no longer understood what she was hearing, as if her mind was floating in a thick liquid, when a cry from the Duce brought her back to reality:

Italians! In a memorable gathering, in Berlin, I said that, according to the laws of fascist morals, when you have a friend you march with him to the end. This we have done and will do with Germany, with its people, with its wonderful armed forces.

Amalia looked up. The faces of the old were dark. For those who had been under Austria, Germany was frightening.

There is only one order. It is categorical and compulsory for everyone. It already wings over, inflaming hearts from the Alps to the Indian Ocean: win! And we will win, to bring a long period of peace with justice, finally to Italy, Europe, the world.

While the radio continued to croak, broadcasting applause and patriotic songs, the younger people rejoiced. Bepi went outside and began to smoke his pipe.

4th April 1941, Travesio.

When the Secretary of the local *Fascio* had entered the café and asked about Ester, Bepi had barely refrained from making a face, but in those days... She had said yes right away. "Daddy, Daddy, I have been made inspector of GIL!" Bepi had not had the heart to rejoice. Ester had sensed it, but she loved him too much to be angry with him.

GIL, the *Gioventù Italiana del Littorio* had been founded in 1937 to replace the *Opera Nazionale Balilla*. It provided sports, military and moral training for the new generations of fascist Italy. You entered GIL aged six and left it at twenty-one to become a member of the National Fascist Party. Jews were excluded from both. The whole programme of the association was in its motto: BELIEVE – OBEY – FIGHT.

That year Ester, who was nineteen, worked as a substitute teacher at the primary school in Travesio. That is why they had thought of her. She would have to work in conjunction with the Secretary of the *Fascio* and with the other teachers to organize the Christmas of Rome, the fascist festival that celebrated the foundation of the Eternal City, on 21st April. Maestro Franzoni would come from Spilimbergo to prepare choirs. On that occasion they would award a prize to the best essays written by sixth year pupils. They had already thought about the topic: *Why I love the Duce!*

11th May 1941, Travesio.

She had immediately liked the young tank crewman who came from far away. For his kindness when he addressed her. For the fineness of his face and hands. For the bold attitude with which he wore his cap sideways. *A nice boy,* she thought.

And then Giulio was good at telling stories... He did not waste the opportunity to tell her about the hotel his family owned in Loiano, about the big house where he lived with his widowed mother. If he wanted to, he could live off their properties, but doing nothing he ran the risk of getting bored. So, once back home he would find a job. His father had been an antiques dealer, mostly as a hobby...

He knew how to do magic tricks with cards, and impersonations. He brought her funny gifts. He stayed a month near Travesio while his regiment, the 31st Tank, was around for the manoeuvres. Then they moved to Pordenone, but he came back to visit her on Sundays, cycling all the way. She could not refuse the courtship of such a nice and decent fellow, who made her laugh and feel important.

3rd August 1941, Travesio.

He remembered only her dress, a shiny green, and the white circles that hung from her ears on that day. It had all happened so fast. "Shit bag of a tank!" shouted an infantry soldier to Giulio, who had responded with a shove. They had been restrained by some comrades. It seemed all over. A scuffle just like so many others, in a village that was full of soldiers.

The square was back to Sunday life. Bikes were passing by. Head-scarfed old ladies went to Mass. In a corner two young girls were playing.

Giulio entered the café with his friends. They began with a glass of wine and then had another. When Ester and her sister returned from Mass on their bikes, Giulio approached them. Ester was beautiful, and she smiled, happy to be loved. He accompanied her into the *contrada*, the alley next to the house.

In the alley it was a stolen kiss. Ester was still laughing and Giulio had eyes only for her: for her soft and smooth hair, for her dress full of sun, for the curve of her breasts, which a shiny fabric barely held back. He could not wait to be her husband.

It was then that they heard the engine. They both turned. In that military truck with its load of young people in uniform there was something they recognised instinctively. Giulio saw the infantry soldier with whom he had tussled. He saw the finger pointed at him, at her.

Giulio took Ester's arm. They entered the house from the back. Outside, voices could be heard.

In the meantime, Giulio's friends had seen the truck arrive. Some had gone out. They had formed two groups, at either side of the square. There was no time to lose.

Giulio explained the situation to Ester's father. He would close the café. The soldiers would calm down.

Bepi had not yet finished closing the shutters when a rock broke a window. He was frozen. Giulio said, "I'm going out!"

The infantry had gathered in front of the café, flanked by two wings of tanker soldiers. They were outnumbered three to one. A gesture, an insult would suffice to escalate things. Anything could happen.

What happened, however, was the unexpected.

With her white circles hanging from her ears, with her shiny dress as green as life, it was she who took a step forward. The one who launched the challenge was Ester. She emerged from the shadows of the bar. She sat in the doorway with her legs apart, her arms against the jambs of the door as a shield between the world and the man she loved, without hesitation, without thinking.

"Come on. Whoever wants to enter must get past me!"

Courage inspires admiration. Confronted with that beautiful girl in a green dress who was so determined, so indifferent to danger, someone made a gesture with his hand, someone else smiled. That was men's business. They had not come there to fight it with women.

"Come on," said one.

The truck driver opened the door: "Come on, we have nothing to do here!"

They got on the truck one by one.

"Let's go to Usago and drink at Carnielutti's!"

"What the fuck are we doing here!"

"Shit bag Tank Corps!" was the last cry they heard from the truck as it drove away.

10th June 1942, Loiano.

He had not set foot in his home village since his father's funeral. Twelve years had passed. And even then Antonio had been back only for a few hours. He loved his father and would never have missed his funeral. His father was the only one who had given him confidence. His mother had not even come to the wedding, with the excuse that Novara was too far.

Not to mention the fact that he had not received a lira from his family. Not a lira to start a new life. Had it not been for Pina's father, who had found him a job and had helped them pay for the furniture...

When they arrived in Bologna, Giulio was there waiting for them. Ester saw him even before the train stopped. She put her head out of the window and shouted "Giulio, Giulio! We are here!" while waving her hand. Her mother, standing behind her, kept an eye on the bags, but such happiness was contagious.

When the two lovers embraced, for a minute even the presence of Amalia did not suffice to detach Ester from her Giulio, who sometimes smiled with mild embarrassment at his future mother-in-law and sometimes was blissfully lost in the smell of the girl he loved.

Giulio had gone whole hog. There was a car waiting for them. The driver, Signor Ariodante, told many anecdotes as they climbed towards Loiano.

Giulio was sitting in front. To be near him, Ester was sitting up behind him, but now she could see only the back of his head, his hair cropped short. Giulio was so well built. He had two well-shaped shoulders and a beautiful neck. And then he was so gentlemanly. You could see that even Ariodante held him in high esteem!

The road became more winding. Amalia had to hold onto the handle above the door. Certainly, Ariodante had a rather reckless way of driving. She had never liked cars. And up those mountain roads! With cliffs on all sides. She resolved to look down as little as possible. After all, she was from the plain. She had been born in Palmanova. And although Travesio was backed by high mountains, still you saw them from down below.

Once they got out of the car, everything looked beautiful to Ester. It is true that in her imagination the house was somehow in better shape, but it was undoubtedly a large building, and then so old.

When Giulio let her in, the moment was solemn. She looked with new eyes at that entrance hall in which she would walk so many times, and the staircase, which she would come to know.

A stern-looking woman watched her from the top of the stairs. For a moment she was afraid of that haughty face. Then she realised that she looked a bit like Giulio, and her fear abated. When the woman in black, with pearl earrings and a long necklace, invited Ester and her mother to come in, she felt that she would get used to her. Perhaps she would never love her mother-in-law, but that woman wanted to be polite: she had opened the door of her house to her.

10th November 1942, Reggio Calabria.

They were fed up with travelling. They had been on that train for two days, without setting a foot down. The troop train was like that. They stopped for hours in a siding. If they did not need them to fight over there, they could have left them in Piedmont, where they were fine! Instead those wagons, filled with the smell of sweat and clogged toilets...

Giulio could not take it any more. They played cards for hours, but his thoughts ran elsewhere. "Blame it on El Alamein! It's Rommel's fault if we are here! It's because of him we have to go to Africa to fight."

"It's not Rommel's fault. If anything it's General Stumme who went on to die in the middle of the battle. And then he was a fool! Rommel though... It's not by mistake that they call him Desert Fox. Had he had it his way we would have slipped a nice suppository up those English and American gentlemen's arses..."

"I say that the fault lies precisely with the British," added another: "the fault for everything. For they care only about oil. And they want to keep Italy under the boot."

"Of course, to think that a place like El Alamein, a cesspool like that... a little station in the middle of the desert. So many people died!"

Once they arrived at the station of Reggio Calabria, the train stopped at the last track. Who knew when it would be leaving?

Two children were playing on the platform. A soldier called them from the window. "Hey, do you want to earn some money?" The soldier pulled out a few coins. "Go and grab me a sandwich and a beer! Keep the rest."

His soldier friends teased him. "You're a silly fool! Your money's gone for good." A few minutes later, however, the kids came back with a sandwich and a beer. It had been a good investment.

Immediately another soldier leaned out the window. And another, and another. The two children took the money and fled, but they were already being called from other parts of the train.

They returned with their arms full of sandwiches and beers. Everyone wanted to eat and drink. It was a chorus of voices.

Other children began to collect coins coming down in showers from the windows. They ran off with the money, and came back with other sandwiches and beers.

They took a new round of orders, but the restaurant of the station had run out of sandwiches. In order not to return the money, the children disappeared.

The soldiers who were parked under the early afternoon sun, inside those little tin boxes, were left with only a small reserve of patience. They would have to be content with that.

Africa

22nd November 1942, Libya.

Giulio enjoyed a certain freedom because he took care of the kitchen. Not that he could cook! He had not even tried. He did not go beyond *miazzole...* But they sent him and another buddy around with a Jeep to look for fruit and vegetables in markets and farms.

Of course he spent all day on the road, but in the end he enjoyed it. He liked meeting people. He always had a joke ready and made friends with everyone. And then while he was looking for supplies he also found the way to get writing paper, the thread that bound him to Italy.

That day a funny thing happened. Instead of going into town to buy fruit, he had the idea to look for it at an oasis that was not far away. So he had begun to trade with the Arabs. He and his partner left the Jeep under the shade of the palm trees and ventured among the camels and the tents. Giulio drew his best smile and made good use of the few words of Arabic he had learned: *salam* or *salam alaikum* to say hello, *shukran* to thank. When he said *shukran*, they answered *afwan* or *ahlan wa sahlan* or other things he did not understand. They were all extremely kind!

Haggling over the price of dates was a long business. They sat in the tent and began with the ritual of tea. A sweet and aromatic tea that Giulio immediately relished. But the price their host asked for the dates was too high. "We Italians poor," said Giulio, turning the pockets of his uniform inside out to show they were empty... Briefly, between laughter and grimaces and raised hands, they returned to the field with a Jeep full of dates. That evening they would celebrate!

2nd December 1942, Libya.

What a difference from the mountains of Piedmont! Since they had landed at the Castel Benito airport, near Tripoli, they had ended up in another world, even if initially the temperature was far from summery. Then things had changed. Since they were not far from the coast, as soon as they could, Giulio and his brothers in arms plunged into the water singing like crazy:

Tripoli, bel suol d'amore,

ti giunga dolce questa mia canzon!

Luckily, where they were it was easy to get something decent to eat, and there was as much water as they wanted. They had heard different stories from those who had fought in Libya for a long time...

The important thing, however, was to reassure Ester and her family. From his letters everything had to look like a holiday. Back home they were certain to worry all the same! So it was better to laugh it off. Or to talk about love... What could he tell Ester that day? Ah, yes!

Ester dearest,

Today we had a really hot day. Fortunately we have a bathroom, and I was able to take two refreshing showers. I am getting as dark as a Moor. I am almost always walking around in a pair of shorts, a vest and beret. You can imagine how cute I am... The British aircraft harassed us often, but they did not cause any harm. On the contrary, I believe that some of them have kicked the bucket, thanks to the valour of our fighters.

Two days ago, in company with a colleague, I bought a gramophone, with a great collection of records (the most recent date from 1940) and in the evening my tent, which is the best in the department and I am not boasting, is brightened up with some music.

When we first meet the Brits, I want to see if I can get myself a radio. It would be very useful, as it would allow us to know all the news and it would make us feel closer to our homeland.

What are you up to? When I listen to the songs that you played so often, I picture myself near you, as in the good times we spent together. You are present inside me at all times and I feel an increasingly powerful desire to bind you to me for ever.

Yours forever,

Giulio

3rd December 1942, Libya.

Strolling in the narrow streets traversed by high arches seemed unreal to Giulio. Houses in the Medina had grates on the windows – so that women could watch without being seen, he was told – and low doorways that opened into dark caverns. In summer it must have been cool in there even when the sun was baking the bricks. In the Arab city everything had been conceived with one eye to the climate.

The place he liked most in Tripoli was Souk el-Turk, the commercial area. In the shady street, which was covered by a trellis hung with vines, men in oriental dress walked beside gentlemen in jackets and hats. It was strange to be in such a faraway place and then read those Italian signs above the shops: *Profumi Orientali, Spezie,* there was even a *Casa del Bebè!* Libya was by now the 'fourth shore' of Italy. Giulio felt proud of the idea that the African city was Italian.

Every few metres, one of the four soldiers stopped in front of a shop to see the piles of colourful spices or to watch a butcher cutting the meat or to admire the gold and silver artefacts, the pottery, the woodwork. It was a new world, which left you open-mouthed...

Giulio thought of Ester. She would have been so happy, had she been there with him.

Suddenly they found themselves in a square that was surrounded by modern buildings. In the centre was a garden. "That is the Arch of Marcus Aurelius," cried Bernardoni. "You see, Tripoli is a very old city! We were here already at the time of the Romans. Libya is part of the empire. We have recovered what was ours!"

Giulio was listening. He had not studied much history, but he had got the idea that at the power of ancient Rome all knees buckled. Was it possible that today's Italy, the Italy of young people like him, was destined to dominate the Mediterranean once again? He swelled with pride. He already felt a citizen of the world, a first-class citizen, who was at home everywhere. Too bad there was a war!

"Come on! We need to go back to Suani," said Bernardoni.

Without knowing why, Giulio found himself full of melancholy. Africa was beautiful, when you were away from the front, but night was approaching. He would have been so happy at home... At home, with his wife. And on a Sunday morning, before going to Mass, they would stroll down the streets of the town. Everybody would be watching her.

23rd December 1942, Libya.

Farewell Tripoli! They moved to the east, in the direction of the front. Luckily Giulio and his fellow soldiers were stationed in Misrata, near the sea, where there was a FIAT truck repair station.

They were camped near Villaggio Crispi. He did not know why, but he was fond of that place. Not that it had anything in particular...

Villaggio Crispi was one of many settlements that had been founded by the Authority for the Colonization of Libya and by the Institute for Social Security. Some villages were named after public figures such as Marconi, Garibaldi and D'Annunzio, while others had even more resounding names, like Villaggio Littoriano. Villaggio Crispi was complete with a church, a town hall, a *Casa del Fascio*, a doctor's surgery, a post office and a market. All around lay hundreds of farms, irrigated thanks to deep wells.

Christmas was approaching and homesickness grew stronger. Perhaps that is why Giulio became attached to the church, the square, the few white buildings that stood in the middle of the flat countryside. Those few houses seemed like a centre, an anchorage.

And then he liked western movies, and the Libyan village – all curves and arches – reminded him of an American mission, with the Indians and the desert all around. Feeling like a film hero did him good. In the end being there   as like playing.

29th December 1942, Libya.

The 31st Tank Regiment of the Armoured Division *Centauro* drew up in columns along the Via Balbia, which went from Tripoli to Tobruk following the coast.

Italo Balbo had died in June 1940, when the anti-aircraft artillery of the San Giorgio ship had shot him down by mistake. Or perhaps on purpose, as someone said.

The Via Balbia was wide and well paved – the only artery that allowed the rapid movement of people and vehicles.

That afternoon the soldiers of the 31st came to a strange monument: the Arch of the Fileni, which Balbo had erected on the border between Tripolitania and Cyrenaica. A huge triumphal arch. Worthy of a Pharaoh.

As he passed under the arch in a Jeep, Giulio looked up. For a moment the imposing structure cast its shadow on him. Then there came the blinding sun.

It was Curcio who explained the meaning of that mausoleum in the middle of nowhere.

"The two bronze figures are the Fileni brothers. Centuries ago there was a struggle between Carthage and Cyrene, which was a Greek colony. To decide the border between the two cities, they found a nice system..."

"And that was?" asked Giulio.

"They decided to stage a race. Two runners set off from Carthage and two from Cyrene. Their meeting point would mark the border. The Fileni were faster, but it brought them no good. The inhabitants of Cyrene complied with the agreement, but they buried the runners alive. The boundary is marked by their graves!"

"Can't believe it!"

"There are so many legends like that. In the Middle Ages, Florence and Siena used a race to agree on a border. There were two knights from the two cities. You had to gallop as fast as possible to gain more ground.

The riders had to leave when the cock crowed, and the legend – which was undoubtedly invented by the Florentines – casts the Sienese in the role of the fool. While the Sienese take a white cock and gorge it with food so that he is in good shape when morning comes, the Florentines take a black cock and stint him. So the next morning the black cock begins to sing before the sun is out, hoping that they will give him something to eat..."

Giulio laughed: "So the Florentines got Chianti, and still drink wine!"

"With our cunning," said Ercoli, "I want to see who wins the war! Down with those treacherous Brits!"

"*Tripoli bel suol d'amore*," attacked Giulio. The word *amore* reminded him of Ester, but the spell was broken by Ercoli, who farted so loudly that everybody started laughing.

When the column stopped, one of the first steps required to set up the camp was the toilets – for if you shit around in the desert you are certain to put your foot in it sooner or later!

11th January 1943, Libya.

Finally they came back to Tripoli. They were based on Tarhuna, twenty-five miles from the sea. Those ten days they had spent in the desert, near the front, he would have gladly forgotten them. They had suffered from thirst. They had known fear. Even if he was lucky, for he belonged to the Repair and Recovery Department and their job was to patch up damaged vehicles, recycle spare parts, salvage what they could.

Those days, however, had left him empty. Those bodies they had extracted from the wreckage and buried in the sand in a hurry, wrapped in a cloth, if there was one... He only dreamed that it would soon end.

15th January 1943, Libya.

When Giulio and his companions – not all of them – returned to Tripoli, he saw the city through different eyes. A month earlier he had admired the Lungomare Conte Volpi, Tripoli's stately waterfront, with its palm trees and columns.

He had dreamed of returning to that city with his pockets full of money, of bringing Ester to the Grand Hotel. He imagined with pleasure the Moorish-style room the young couple would be given. Perhaps they would play at the casino...

When he had first seen Tripoli, the port, with its majestic warships, had seemed grandiose. He had stopped with his friends to watch the unloading of a German anti-tank cannon. They had followed attentively while the heavy weapon was hoisted on a pontoon and placed on the ground.

Everything had changed, however. The city was no longer the same. Bombs fell from the sky. The enemy was approaching. Everything was scarce. Was it possible that Italians were destined to lose Tripoli?

4th May 1943, Travesio.

What had she said? – thought Bepi – *You forget even your children.* It was not true! Bepi looked up at the sky. White clouds drifted above the fields and hills, just like his thoughts. And the warm air of that spring afternoon filled his lungs with a joy which he had not known since long ago.

The world was celebrating that glorious sunny day. The river water was celebrating – the clear water at which he had looked with longing while passing over the bridge – and the flowers in the meadows, and the green grass, as green as life in its best season. And even if he was no longer young, life continued to be green in his eyes while he was riding his bike in Laves, beyond the river and the houses, along the country road which ran at the foot of the hills, towards a place that was so dear to him.

Far from Amalia, he was about to say, but he was not angry with her. Only, they were so different at times, and while she had eyes for everything at home and she was always ready to do the right thing, he had to wander with his head. Yes, he had to open the doors of his mind to the great space that surrounded him and pressed upon him with its breath, asking to be recognised.

He had with him his colours and the plywood on which to paint. There was no need for an easel. There is always something to lean on in the midst of nature. Nature gives you everything. He knew this, and there was nothing else he needed.

He turned down a side road. Here was the Puntič. He knew where to abandon those two wheels and where to position himself so that the bridge would appear in its dark beauty: the deep cleft between two rocks that the stone arch – older than memory – united as an outrage to the principle of gravity. Those stones which over the centuries had resisted the temptation of matter: falling into the bottom of the crevasse, drowning with a thud in the water, which kept waiting, enigmatic and treacherous, with its mumbling, with its green swirling, with its lazy shadows.

And then, beyond the bridge, beyond that suspended miracle, beyond the idea that had been thrown over to join two rocky shores, the other miracle: that lake of peace, that mirror of emerald water, that happy crystal, the colour of trees and of hope. This was the place he loved, where he was alone with his thoughts, away from home, from people, from the military trucks that passed by at all hours, from the uniforms.

There he was alone with his colours – the colours of nature and the colours which he extracted from his wooden box, which he mixed on his palette, like a magician or perhaps a demigod.

How many years had passed since he had attended the Academy of Fine Arts in Venice? Sometimes he thought he had failed. There were days when he wondered what he had done with his life. Travesio. Then that name sounded alien, as alien to him as that small village wedged in a corner of the plain between the hills and the mountains – San Giorgio and the Ciàurleč, the two guardians of the valley, one small and one tall, but so is beauty.

Beauty is in the irregularity of things, in their defects, in their being as they are.

There were days when he would have wanted not to be there, but other times he thought of his brother Memi, who worked in Venice, in an insurance company, and he realised he was lucky. At least he was in contact with those mountains and valleys, and those corn fields in which he could lose himself. He glanced towards the bell tower of the church, the tip of which he saw behind the trees. He thought of the chapel that he had finished decorating a month earlier. Little jobs that enabled him to live. Then there was the café, and Amalia. In the café there were more and more Germans.

He put the plywood on a big stone he knew, against a tree trunk he knew. On the plywood a replica of that landscape: the two shoulders of rock and the arch of the bridge, but among them – above and below the bridge – the void. A hazy but optimistic void: a bright white background, with a touch of cadmium yellow, which Bepi had prepared at home.

He knew what light effect he wanted to obtain and he began to spread on that dry yet liquid background the colours he saw before him. He arranged his palette and the brush began to dance.

Perhaps he would actually sell that painting to the pharmacist, who had already asked for it. Or perhaps he would keep it for himself. He did not know. Meanwhile, he would beat the pharmacist at chess that night. He had to show him, since the night before the pharmacist had checkmated him in a few moves.

From the milky background a steep lawn took shape, little by little, besieged by branches. Maybe he would put a swan in the lake...

He was interrupted by a bicycle bell. "Daddy, Daddy! I'm going down to Usago to buy some bread. There's none to be found in Travesio. I like the idea of a bike ride."

"Be careful! It may rain," he said looking at the clouds that were gathering on the horizon. And off Ester went, always in a hurry.

He lit his pipe and stopped to look at the blue sky on which a grey wall of clouds hung in the distance. It seemed to him his life was in that sky. He relished his tobacco, like a wise man from the East smoking his hookah, looking at things from a distance, savouring every single moment.

Ester, Delia, Ennio. There were the children. How could she say that he did not think of them! This was not the future he had dreamed of. He dreamed of a united Europe, of a world without borders, a better world, but there was death. The omnipresent death, the senseless death that he could not shake out of his life and out of his painting. The dying swan.

He remembered a time when he could not sleep, when he was tormented by the thought of death. He had left the room and had found himself in the kitchen, sitting at the table, his head in his hands. He was in spasms, suffering the unspeakable pain of not seeing beyond the threshold of unconsciousness, of silence. He had sought help from God, but God had not answered. Then he had turned to the lesser god he felt closer to him than God the Father – his own father.

He had asked for a sign, with the certainty of despair, with the blind strength of those who have nothing to lose. His senses had been struck by the sound of a click. The light had gone off and on three times. And then he had believed. He had believed to tears, and for a while he had no longer been afraid of death. And he had never again been so afraid of death, ever. Death had been vanquished.

The clouds were down there, in the background. He put his pipe on the grass, picked up the brush and began to paint the water of the lake.

7th May 1943, Bologna.

When Veronica met Signora Nicoli they understood each other straight away. Because they both felt things others could not sense. This happened to Veronica when she least expected it. That night she had dreamed of her grandmother Benizia. Granny was badly dressed, her hair all dishevelled. She worried about Giulio. Veronica had woken up with a start. She could no longer sleep. What did that dream mean?

As soon as she could, she knocked on the door of her friend's house. They lived close by.

Signora Nicoli made coffee. Then she took out her pendulum, a photograph of Giulio, and a map of North Africa. She put the photograph on the table while holding the pendulum, which began to spin clockwise.

The woman put her finger on the map, right on the word Tripoli. The pendulum reversed direction. "You see. He is no longer in Libya."

"That's what Giulio's girlfriend wrote to me. He's now in Tunisia."

Signora Nicoli moved her finger to Tunis. The pendulum resumed turning clockwise. "Yes, he's in Tunis."

"Who knows what's going on! In my dream, my grandmother was all upside down."

Signora Nicoli moved the pendulum again over the photo of Giulio. She asked if he was alive. The pendulum spun clockwise. She asked if he was well. Clockwise again. She asked if he was in danger. The pendulum reversed direction.

"Don't worry, dear. Destiny is never written in advance! He may well be unscathed."

When Veronica came home to prepare dinner, Cleto said: "Oh, what a terrible day for our troops down in Africa. They said it on the radio: The British have taken Tunis."

25th June 1943, Travesio.
Ester was coming out of the alley riding her bike when in the distance she saw a waving arm. It was the post woman, who was already shouting: "Here's Giulio!" She dropped the bike and ran towards her. She had not heard from Giulio for some time. She knew of the Italian defeat in Africa, and every day she feared the arrival of bad news.

Her joy left place to dismay. What was written on the top of the card left no space for doubt: PRISONER OF WAR POST CARD.

The address had also changed: *Sender's Name NA / T 1032 Sergente Maggiore Ascari Giulio – Regio Esercito – POW 211 – Information Bureau – Provost – General Marshall, Washington DC USA*

What did that address mean? What was Giulio doing in America? She read the message:

9th June 1943

Dear Ester,
I cannot describe the joy I feel at being able to send you my news. I am happy to assure you that I am enjoying good health and I feel great. Sometimes I read novels, to my great delight. Too bad that they can be rarely found, but we usually play chess and draughts and I am a true champion, so much so that I have earned the title of unbeatable. Please do not worry about me and give my news to Mum, Veronica and Cleto. When you write to me, please use this address and send it also to my Mother. I guess you've all suffered because of me and I want to assure you that my thoughts are always with you. I send my warmest greetings to your dear Mum, your Dad, Delia and

*Ennio, and I hope to hear from you soon. I kiss you and hug you with
immense love.*

Yours forever
Giulio

Ester showed the card to her father, but Bepi did not
understand, so they addressed an officer who was in the café.
"But why have they taken him to America?" asked Ester, who was
desperate at the idea that a whole ocean divided her from Giulio.

"Eh, who knows where your boyfriend is? He could be in
America or Africa or somewhere else. Don't be alarmed. With the
Americans he's not in bad hands."

Falling Bombs

8th September 1943, Travesio.

In the café they were all waiting next to the radio. At 7.42 pm, speaking from the microphones of *EIAR*, Maresciallo Badoglio announced that he had asked General Eisenhower for an armistice. The request had been granted. Every act of hostility should cease everywhere. Those dry words, uttered in a broken voice, hurt.

People began to argue. The pharmacist commented: "News of the armistice has already been given also by Radio Algiers. And now you've heard Badoglio."

"But what does this mean?" exclaimed Bepi. "Is it the end of the war? Will they continue to fight?"

"And the King, why is he not heard?"

"And Mussolini, where's Mussolini?"

"We'll regret this. The Germans will call us to account!"

"Perhaps it was the only thing Badoglio could do."

"Who knows what's coming next?" wondered an old man.

18th September 1943, Travesio.

"Switch on the radio. Mussolini's speaking on the radio!" The pharmacist entered the café without greeting anyone. He was speaking in a loud voice, waving his arms. Everyone fell silent. A man switched on the radio and began to turn the knob. The radio croaked out. A song. Some classical piece. The voice of the Duce. They did not know when the talk had started. They did not know from where he spoke.

"It's Radio Monaco," someone said.

I am more convinced than ever – thundered Mussolini – *that the House of Savoy wanted, prepared and organized, even to the last detail, the coup, with the complicity of Badoglio, who performed it, but also of certain cowardly generals.*

Mussolini spoke with contempt for the monarchy, which had planned to deliver him to the enemy, throwing the country into chaos. *When a monarchy fails its responsibilities, it loses any reason for its existence*, he exclaimed, and he reminded Italians of the role Republican leader Giuseppe Mazzini had played in the unification of the country.

In the café people had downcast eyes. They were all serious, especially when Mussolini began to expound his plan: to take up arms on the side of Germany and Japan, to reorganize the armed forces, to do away with traitors.

The speech ended with these words: *Long live Italy! Long live the Fascist Republican Party!* Italy was becoming a Republic, but Mussolini spoke from Munich, in Germany. What did it mean, this return of Mussolini? What would happen to the people of Italy?

25th September 1943, Bologna.

The alarm sounded in the late morning. The priest of the Mascarella church remembered it well. The bombing had surprised him while he was in the *Arcivescovado* building, behind the cathedral, talking with his superiors. As soon as he could leave the air raid shelter, he came striding towards Via Mascarella, looking at the ravages of war. But the worst was yet to come.

His church. At first, he had eyes only for the altar that was sticking out from the rubble. For that space which was so small compared with the immensity of the sky. He kept running from one corner to the other, indifferent to danger, in an attempt to save what he could. But there was little to be saved in that rectangle of land surrounded by high walls. Some candlesticks. The altar cloths. The panels of the *Via Crucis*. He collected each object with feverish anxiety. He was helped by the sexton, who kept saying: "What an awful job! Woe to us!"

He struggled with blind willpower to preserve what remained of his church after that hour of divine judgement. Then he saw the face of Christ who watched him from behind the altar and he understood. His place at that time was not there, but among his people.

He told the sexton to take care of everything and he came running out, not knowing where he was going. He had to see every house in the parish. He had to rescue those in need. His heart would guide him.

After turning the corner of the street, he beheld the void where a house had been. In that pile of rubble was only silence.

How many times had he climbed that staircase? He thought of the families who lived there and whom he knew. Of the Easter blessings. Of the weddings. Of the christenings.

His church did not matter. His church existed for his people. People were the treasure that God had given him. It was them that Jesus had asked him to love. Life went on. As long as there was a child. As long as there was an old man. As long as there was someone to help.

Somebody called his name. He did not have time to turn when a woman threw herself into his arms. The arms of a priest. It did not matter at that time. It did not matter in the least that he was a man and she was a woman. That they were in the middle of a street.

He held her close. He felt her breast against his chest. He felt her tears bathe his neck. He heard that word again: "My husband, my husband... He was alive. I talked to him."

There were enough churches. Christ had no need of a roof. At that moment he was there, with him and the woman, and suffered with them for that death which was also his death.

4th October 1943, Travesio.

As GIL inspector, Ester was asked to collect the uniforms that had been handed out to young girls. She tried to knock on a few doors, but no one heeded her. Then she realised that she had better leave the matter alone. Times were hard and people were far from ready to give up a dress. And then the time had ended when everybody pretended to be a fascist. A few days earlier she had heard her father speak to the pharmacist. They spoke of civil war.

She did not understand anything about politics and did not bother to. When she received letters from Udine with the symbol of the *Fascio*, sometimes she did not even open them, or if she opened them she did not answer. She liked gatherings, singing. She was convinced she looked pretty wearing a uniform.

The next day she would turn twenty-two. But there was a war and Giulio was far away, a prisoner in Africa. What a time to be young! Then there was hunger. In cities it was worse, but even in the countryside they only just had enough to eat.

She thought of the time – she was still a young girl – when she had stolen a whole salami. She had never told her mother that it had been her.

One day Amalia had noticed that a salami was gone from the cellar. She had gone up to the kitchen and had asked the children. No one knew anything.

Bepi would not bother to take notice of such things. According to him, she had made a mistake while counting. Amalia certainly made no mistake while counting, but she let it go. She knew her three children were young. Although food at table was not lacking, there was never too much.

16th October 1943, Travesio.

"I tell you, now it's the Germans who are in control, not the fascists!" Even in Travesio those posters had appeared on the street walls. On top, the German eagle and swastika. At the bottom, a signature: *The Supreme Commissioner: Dr Rainer.*

"And the Social Republic?" asked Bepi.

"The Social Republic covers another part of Northern Italy, but this area is under the Germans. We are part of the Reich."

"It's called Operational Zone of the Adriatic Littoral," added another: "Goodbye Italy, you know? We have gone back to the time of the Austrians. Only, this time it is not the Austrians who are in command, but the Germans."

"For us it's over. We are in Germany now." While the man spoke, his hands were shaking. "Poor Friuli!" he added, and after drinking what remained of his grappa, he left the room.

7th December 1943, Monte Ciaurlec̆.

The Garibaldi Brigade Friuli had moved up there after the Germans had started to round up Italian men in November. Young people arrived in the mountains almost every day.

Ettore had lost his faith as a child and believed in a secular anti-fascism. He had joined the Garibaldi because he wanted to fight the Nazis. To see the Wehrmacht rule the roost in Udine made his blood boil. So here he was up in the mountains, where you died of cold, and you had to fight to save your skin and to get back under a roof at night.

They slept in huts nobody used in winter, in the barns of farmers, who more or less willingly gave them something to eat when he and the others knocked at their door. It was not comfortable, the life of a partisan. You risked being hated by everybody because you could not work. Luckily mountain people understood that what partisans were doing was important. Or it would be soon.

Ettore had studied at the university. And he had brought with him two books, both by Dostoyevsky. He had taken them from his bedroom without thinking. Only afterwards had he wondered why those. One was *Crime and Punishment*. It was about the fine line that exists between fighting for an ideal and ending up being blinded by your own ideas. When Raskolnikov kills the usurer, he thinks that he will use her money to do good. Then he realises that his act has already taken him too far. You cannot build a better humanity without respect for human beings. Ettore knew it was a difficult law. Also because for him it was not tinged with weeping Madonnas and angels sitting on clouds. It was an entirely mundane law, in which he believed as a man. Not as a Christian.

The other book he had brought was *The Brothers Karamazov*. There was a chapter that he always would remember, a story that Ivan Karamazov tells his brother Alexei. We are in Spain, at the time of the Inquisition. Christ returns to earth and is acclaimed by the people, but the Inquisitor condemns him to death, and also explains why.

Because Christ, with his message of love and poverty, lays the emphasis on everybody's freedom, while people are not able to live free. People, as the Inquisitor claims, need authority, somebody who uses power to satisfy their material needs and answer their doubts. This is the function of the Church: bringing order to society and our souls, but Christ... Christ was a revolutionary.

Reading those pages was important for Ettore. His insights had been confirmed and had developed. He was now able to touch the invisible cages in which individuals were confined. By telling you how to behave, propaganda – be it the Church's or the regime's – gave you the peace of those who sleep or who are prisoners. He wanted to reason with his head. He would never ask anyone to think for him.

He was not an anarchist, but he had read Errico Malatesta and he agreed with him. Religious power was used to control men, numbing intelligence and feelings. He just could not believe that the Church knew word for word what God wanted from men. It sufficed to read a few books to work out where the Church stood. It sufficed to see how it had behaved in recent years, kneeling before the fascists.

He could not bring Dostoyevsky with him when he was in action. But he knew that his two books were in that mountain hut, on a shelf, where you could not see them if you did not know. And where he could find them each time he returned. His home was there. The home of the ideas he had to go back to not to lose the sense of things, not to let blood get him drunk, not to become like the enemy. He did not want to have anything in common with Germans and fascists. Nothing at all.

Christmas 1943, Novara.

It was cold in those days and Pina walked fast. Her fingers were frozen, despite the gloves. Even her breath froze. Suddenly her attention was attracted by a Red Cross poster: PARCEL SHIPPING to PRISONERS in GERMANY.

There were three kinds of five pound packs. Clothing packs contained a sweater, four pairs of woollen socks, two girdles, a balaclava, four handkerchiefs, two items of woollen underwear, two tank tops, and loose tobacco. One was advised to fill food parcels with dried apricots, sugar, condensed milk, jam, biscuits, and then tinned meat, stock cubes, soap. There was also a mixed pack with food, clothing, tobacco and vitamin C.

Pina felt overcome by sadness. Poor people! What had they done wrong? They needed everything. Once she got home she would jot down the list. Depending on what she found, she would prepare a package and take it to the Red Cross after Christmas.

She resumed walking, not as briskly as before. A hazy sunshine seemed to filter through the fog.

29th January 1944, Bologna.

The raids had been going on for months. So many things had happened, but the disaster seemed to have no end. This time the alarm sounded on a late Saturday morning. Those who had run to shelters still heard the roars. Some prayed in front of makeshift altars. Others ate. Those who had not lost their appetite. Those who had something with them.

One could breathe death and destruction in the air. When the alarm was over, a little after one o'clock, they came out from cellars and basements. The dust had not settled yet.

Fine Arts Superintendent Barbacci ran to the city centre. He wanted to see everything, to know everything. Everywhere he met desolation. It had taken centuries of art, centuries of history, to build what modern aircrafts could destroy in a few minutes. Humanity had never seemed so barbaric. He knew he should weep for lives before palaces and churches, but his thoughts turned to his proud Bologna, to the ancient brick city, which was slowly crumbling under the impact of war.

When he arrived in Piazza Santo Stefano someone told him that a little further on there was some serious damage. He hurried on.

The arcades before the *Teatro del Corso* were mutilated. A mountain of rubble had invaded the street. Inside, what remained of the theatre hall were two tiers of boxes, part of the stage. Huge beams and piles of tiles and bricks and wooden planks littered the parterre, along with delicious wrecks. Fine ornaments. White and gilded stuccoes. Crystal pendants from broken lamps. Strips of red velvet. Tattered red curtains with gold fringes.

That space of artificial lights, declaiming voices, resounding applause and frivolous worldly life was reduced to ruins. The performance had been cancelled at one stroke in the few hours which separated an everyday morning from that afternoon of sadness.

A clear blue sky mocked his pain. Life went on. Vanity. Only vanity. He felt a burden on his heart. All the rules of his existence had to be rewritten. Poor mad humanity. Poor little human beings who strive and toil and worry and hope and fear. Poor creatures who are powerless in the face of destiny, which one day can crush you like insects. Before you have time to wonder why.

17th February 1944, Travesio.

The pharmacist added in a low voice: "I tell you the other night they were also seen in Travesio! Until now, they were up there at Castelnuovo, but now they're here."

Bepi did not know what to think. He was playing chess with the pharmacist and the priest. In the café there was no one besides them.

The priest said nothing, but his face was serious. Bepi instead replied: "They told me about these soldiers with large cloaks and on their heads caps with a red star. People are afraid of them, but nobody knows who they are."

"They're Slavs! It's Tito who sent them," said the pharmacist.

The priest was still silent. And this time Bepi also fell silent. He had never been interested in politics, but he was afraid for Ester.

He still remembered the day when she had gone around the houses to ask for the uniforms back. The very best time to remind everyone that she was a GIL Inspector! But you could not have a discussion with Ester. She was like that, even as a child. *Voglio, posso e comando – I want, I can and I command.* This is what his wife said when she spoke of her. She never saw any obstacles. She had so much courage and seemed to split open the mountains, but she was actually a little girl, unable to appreciate the consequences of her actions.

"People disappear in the night," continued the pharmacist after a long silence. "They say that in Trieste the Slavs throw the Italians into ravines. Is it possible? I find it hard to believe! But then, these days everything is possible."

The priest crossed himself: "God's will be done," but the pharmacist, who did not go to church, even though he played chess with Don Diomede, could not resist: "God, God, God. Don't sell me that. If God exists, it means he's looking the other way!" And putting on his coat he said good night to everyone.

26th February 1944, Novara.

Antonio was shaving his beard, still in his vest, when the bell rang. He heard Pina opening the door. Looking out from the bathroom he saw a soldier. Pina had turned white. Antonio felt his legs tremble.

"Are you Antonio Ascari?"

The soldier pulled out a sheet from his folder and asked him to sign it. Then he left.

One look at the notice sufficed: "I have to report to the German Command. To be enlisted."

"It's not possible!" said Pina, ripping the card out of his hand. "It must be a mistake. Your factory is protected."

"You're right," said Antonio. "We work for the Germans. I'll run to the cotton mill and show the notice to Marotti. You'll see. I'm sure he'll talk to the proper authorities. The notice must have been sent out to all workers, but there's factory and factory."

They parted.

Pina was teaching music at school, but her head was elsewhere. She was pursuing questions that were all different and yet all the same.

Will he have to leave?

When will it happen?

Will he come back?

Will I lose him?

Tomorrow will I be crying or laughing?

What will my future be?

Shall we both see the end of the war?

Will I wear black?

Will I be happy?

When she got home she felt as if she had covered an impossibly long distance on foot. She had no energies left. She was waiting for the door to open. She looked forward to seeing his face. She would read the truth behind each mask.

The time came. She heard the key turn. She ran into the hall. Antonio put his hat on the console table with a nonchalant gesture, almost playfully. He looked at her and smiled. It was a true, spontaneous smile, expressing the joy of life.

Pina felt a weight slipping from her chest. She gave a deep sigh, and Antonio was already holding her.

"Eight people received the notice in the cotton mill, but the director told us not to worry. None of us can be enlisted because the plant has been exonerated by the *Fabbriguerra* Ministry."

Pina was also smiling now.

"Marotti made a phone call. We all heard it because we were in his office. He said that he absolutely cannot do without us. When I went out with the others, it didn't seem real... I've always said that he's a good person."

27th February 1944, Novara.

After Antonio had returned home and given her the news, she felt so light. As if she had lost ten years and ran on the wings of the wind. Nothing burdened her.

On Sunday morning, she had prepared the best things she could find. In the afternoon they had gone to see a romantic movie. It was like going back to the first months of marriage, as if life had started again. Only occasionally a restlessness possessed her.

28th February 1944, Novara.

At night she had bad dreams. The next morning, however, waking up next to him, she regained contact with reality. And then Antonio's confidence was contagious. There was nothing to worry about.

It was when Antonio came home in the afternoon that the glass shattered. And the fragments were scattered where it was no longer possible to collect them. She heard it from the way he turned the key, from the way he closed the door behind him, from the silence. Pina left the kitchen and saw his eyes.

Antonio ran up to her and squeezed her until it hurt. She felt his sobs shake his chest. She did not have the strength to ask, not even to cry. She froze. Her body had understood what her mind could not admit.

Antonio began to rub his head in the crook of her shoulder. He pressed against her with an animal gesture of love. She took his head in her hands. She looked at him with eyes full of sweetness, as if her soul had melted.

When Antonio was sitting in the kitchen and holding her hands, he began to speak: "I found out this morning when I arrived at work. We were told that we had to go to the Command, to clarify. I understood right away that things were not looking good. I cannot tell you in what state the others are. Think of Sborgi, who has kids. At the Command they did not even let us open our mouth. They placed us in a corridor to wait. Then we were given a medical. Able and enlisted."

Tears began to trickle down Pina's face.

"Tomorrow I won't have to work. I have to report on Wednesday with my suitcase, ready to leave. We have a day to spend together."

A single day to spend together, thought Pina. 29th February. A day that somehow did not exist.

She would pack his suitcase that evening. Everything was clean. Until that time, however, life was theirs. Only that day existed. They would live in the present with all the intensity of their love. It was the only chance they had.

"What if instead of reporting you ran away?" she asked.

"To go where? Who do I know that can hide me? And what would I do? Should I reach the partisans? Can you see me being a partisan? I don't even know how to shoot. And I'm almost forty." Antonio shook his head.

Pina wanted to tell him: *and if we went away together?* But Switzerland was so far away. A madness!

There was only that day. "What shall we do tomorrow?" she asked.

"Let's get away from Novara. I don't want to see anyone. Nobody."

29th February 1944, Novara.

Early in the morning the sky was cloudy, then it cleared. They left the city on foot, to leave everything behind.

After a while they left the main road and took a path lined with tall poplars. They wanted to go to one of their places. They wanted a memory to hold onto in the solitude that was waiting for them. Walking did him good. The silence was no longer tense. There was a sweetness in that February day.

They had lunch in a small restaurant they knew. They walked along an embankment. They did not speak. They felt each other with their fingers. They stopped on a small bridge. It was a long hug, a painful kiss. They savoured their smells. They wanted to melt into each other, right there, in that cold and sunny countryside. They wanted to become one, to merge their bodies so that no one could separate them.

Antonio had the idea of jumping into the canal while clinging to her. Dying together. He felt his coat soak with water and drag him to the bottom. He felt his arms tighten around her to prevent her from going back to life, until she herself stopped fighting.

They remained embraced on top of the bridge.

They made love only when they got home. Out of despair. When he came inside her, Pina began to cry.

Lili Marleen

4th March 1944, Berlin.

The great Reich welcomes you. These were the words Antonio heard while passing through the iron gate that marked the transition from one prison – the train to which he had been confined for days – to another prison, the whole of Germany.

The loudspeaker kept reciting its litany, in an Italian that was stained by German sounds: *All acts of sabotage or refusal to work will be punished as a desertion. The companies in which you will be employed will issue you with a new identity card, an Ausweiss.*

He did not have time to wonder what was in store for them in that place when reality caught up with him.

The man who was standing in front of him was so weak that he lost the grip on his suitcase, which fell down. The man knelt to pick it up. A moment later he was lying on the ground. He had been hit by a guard with the butt of his rifle. An act without reason.

Antonio knew that his world was over. In this new world nothing had a reason.

The man was still on the ground while the guard ordered the others to move forward. Antonio lost sight of him. He had spoken with him on the train.

How many other faces would he lose sight of? He wanted to turn around but he did not. He had to survive. He had to return.

Suddenly he felt himself falling into a deep pit: his legs no longer supported him. At that moment the line of prisoners stopped and he was able to rest his shoulder against a wall.

When he opened his eyes, he thought with joy that no one had seen him. Henceforth his joys would be like that: being able to breathe, to feel the plaster of a wall with his fingers, knowing that he was alive and that perhaps, one day, he would return to his world.

7th April 1944, Werneuchen, north-east of Berlin.

That day they were allowed to take their first shower. Antonio and his companions were full of lice. They had got them on the freight train in which they had travelled. Forty or fifty men crammed inside each wagon, sleeping on the straw. Antonio could still remember the smell of the train. He remembered the light coming from the slit between the wall and the door, open just enough to enable them to piss or shit.

He remembered the faces pressed against that opening. Looking out was in itself a luxury, as if stocking up those landscapes, those last impressions of their country, could help them survive in the distance of time.

"Today they'll shave our hair," said a fellow prisoner. "Just as well, I'm fed up with scratching."

They made them strip naked. In the room there was a mirror. Antonio saw himself. He looked so thin. He had spent a little over a month in Germany. What would become of him? Of course with fifteen grams of margarine per day... Perhaps things would improve. Perhaps the war would be soon over. You had to think for the better. Whatever happened, one should never lose hope.

20th May 1944, Werneuchen.

"*Badoglio Scheisse,*" shouted a man on a motorcycle while Antonio and his companions walked escorted back from work. By now he knew that with these words the Germans did not just mean *Badoglio shit*, but *Italians shit* since for them Italians were all traitors. That day, however, it did not matter because that day he would be allowed to write again. His wife had already received news. Now it was his mother's turn.

There was still light when he sat at a table by the barracks' window. On the *Postkarte* he wrote the address where his mother could send something from Italy: Flugplatzkommando A 44/III Werneuchen 2 = Berlin. No question of telling the truth. He would pretend that everything was fine.

Dearest Mother,

I received your two letters. Thank you so much! Now I've changed my address. I'm fine, and if you could send me a parcel you should arrange with Pina to send me work clothes, which are the only things I need. But if all goes well in August I'll get a 10-day licence and then I can take with me what you have got ready. What you tell me of Giulio makes me happy. A good sign! Very good, and very well. Remember me to Cleto and kiss Veronica for me. A flower for Dad on my behalf. A strong hug and fond kisses to you.

Antonio

He had managed to get his hands on a postcard of *Heidelberg im Frühling*, with the river and the bridge and the castle, and a beautiful flowered tree in the foreground. It was spring, wasn't it? He put the two *Postkarten* in the envelope.

With an indescribable longing he thought that those rectangles of paper would travel to where he could not go back – through Germany and the Alps and the plain, down to Bologna, along the road that led to his village. He found himself caressing the envelope with his fingers. While he was sealing it with his saliva, it seemed to him that a piece of his heart would go forth with it.

12th June 1944, Travesio.

It was nearly dark when Amalia saw her two nephews enter the door of the café. She realised immediately that it was something serious. And given what had happened six months before, she feared the worst.

"It's Mum. They took away Mum," said the older nephew, who was fourteen, while the younger one held his hand, a little behind him.

Amalia could not cry in front of them. And she could not say anything in front of the people who were in the café.

"Come, come with me," she said, pushing the boys towards an inner door. Then she addressed her husband, who was watching a group of men playing cards: "Bepi! Bepi! Come here. You stand at the counter."

As he approached, she added in a low voice: "They have taken Luisa."

Bepi's face stiffened.

"Tell me everything," said Amalia when she and her nephews were alone in the back room.

"We heard somebody knock. Mother went to the window. They told her that they would take her to see Dad." The boy stopped speaking.

Amalia could not believe that her sister-in-law had to end up like that. For she knew that she would not come back, but she said nothing. She shut her thoughts inside herself with a double lock. She did not think either of the future or of the past. She asked the boys if they were hungry, but they had already eaten. Amalia could not send those two poor kids home, those two poor... She pushed back the word. *Shut up! Shut up!*

Ester came into the room with Delia. Amalia said only: "They've taken your aunt!"

Under the guise of preparing the bed, she left her nephews with her daughters and went upstairs. Her hands folded the bedspread, opened the drawers, spread the sheets. Her mind was elsewhere.

On the verge of tears, she thought of her brother Bartolo, who had disappeared one night in late January, with his friend Giordano. It was Giordano's son who had told her about that winter night. Those men had come at half past nine. There were three of them. They had asked Giordano to accompany them to Bartolo's for they did not know where he lived. Both Giordano and Bartolo had vanished.

Weeks later, the partisans knocked on the doors of the two families. They asked for clothes, for food, for money, claiming that the two men needed them. Nobody at home could know for certain what they all feared – that Giordano and Bartolo had already died.

Luisa came to see her sister-in-law and cried.

She repeatedly went to the German Command to ask for information. Perhaps they believed she was a spy. Perhaps they thought she was crazy. Perhaps she was only a nuisance.

At that moment she heard the sound of footsteps. It was Bepi: "Now they've taken Dirce away as well." She was Giordano's wife.

They had already tried to take her away a few days before. She was crossing the bridge, when two men approached her. She had clung to the railings, she had begun to scream, but no one had found the courage to approach.

She had been saved because – after a minute that had seemed endless – one of her children, hearing her cries, had run across the square and brought her back with him. Amalia and Ester had seen the whole scene from the window. Dirce believed she had got away with it.

First the husbands, then the wives. Amalia felt tears rolling down her face. Only then was she certain that she would never see her brother and sister-in-law again. With boundless sadness, Bepi took her in his arms.

28th June 1944, Werneuchen.

At the factory, they were not allowed to speak to German workers. Antonio could not possibly have done that anyway because he did not know a word of German, and even after a few months he had not learned much. How could you learn the language of the people who had taken your life away? Who used you as an animal.

On his way to work he walked with his shoulders drooping, looking down. At times he was lost in the sky, as if looking for something, but then his head went down again and he saw nothing except for the grey tarmac, as grey and shapeless as his days.

Then they came into that shed. He worked in the ward next to the Germans, but an invisible wall separated him from them. And even if he had been able to speak their language, what could he say? *I hate you!*

They communicated with the department head through an interpreter. An Italian who knew German. Even among Italians, on the job they had to be careful to use as few words as possible. Otherwise they would be punished.

He hated the canvas that passed through his hands. He could not believe that he had been brought there to do that. Not to produce parachutes and tents and uniforms for the army. What he made were tablecloths, towels, sheets. Objects that would enter the homes of ordinary people. He who no longer had a home.

It was not the work itself that cost him. It is true the rounds were heavy. They worked twelve hours a day, except on Sundays, and once a week they had to do the night shift, but that was not the worst. You had to kill time somehow.

It just did not seem real. Day after day he could not resign himself to believe that this was reality, his life, an invisible life next to that of ordinary people. He had to sit at a certain table, eat certain food, use a certain toilet. In the textile factory, Italians lived a life apart, a few metres from the Germans.

His illness eventually turned into nausea. One day he ended up feeling really bad and fell to the ground. He awoke with a fellow prisoner slapping him. That evening dysentery began. Some crap that he had eaten.

Where was his life? Real life? Where had he lost the thread of his existence?

10th September 1944, Bologna.

Under the bombings the city of Bologna had suffered and struggled. In the centre and on the outskirts there were rips and rubble everywhere. Via Lame was a mass of debris. The train station was but an empty shell, surrounded by twisted shelters and craters filled with stagnant water.

To survive, people made do. They even stocked farmyard animals in the loggias and balconies of palaces. Poverty was so widespread that on the walls one could read notices like this:

Italian Social Republic

Prefecture of Bologna

Notice

Anyone who is caught looting or plundering in areas of the province that have been affected by air raids will be immediately put to death.

With the blackout, the streets were enveloped in total darkness. Only inside homes was there light, but you had to be careful not to let it filter out. At stake was not only your life but that of others.

Those who no longer had a home slept in shelters, and those who still had one ran down to the shelters when the alarm sounded. Then the dance of fear began. Distant sounds. Vibrations. A sudden roar. Dust filtering into the shelter. A bomb had fallen nearby.

Clouds and fog, up in the sky, were friendly companions. Below them the city was busy during the day and could rest peacefully at night.

Many had fled from Bologna. A few days before, however, everything had changed. On 7th September the old town of

Bologna had been declared *Sperrzone* and was protected from both armies and bombing. Bologna was an open city. German soldiers could no longer enter it, although two companies of fascist Black Brigades kept watch on the neighbourhoods.

The flow of civilians reversed. It was now Bologna that attracted people from the countryside, especially from the villages that were close to the front. At the gates of the old city the *Feld Gendarmerie* controlled the traffic of carts, often loaded with household goods. They were the only permitted means of transport in addition to trams. Even riding a bike was forbidden.

When Antenesca insisted on returning to Bologna, at first Teresa did not want to go, but in her condition she had to rely on her. So they left Teresa's country home and returned to Via Castiglione. It mattered little where they stayed. Teresa was ready for anything, but she was sorry for Antenesca, who was still young.

Once in Bologna, Antenesca sounded happier. Teresa heard her singing. She began to suspect that behind the change of scenery there was a love affair.

The Germans still held the city, but you already breathed the air of defeat. Or freedom!

15th September 1944, Loiano.

Lucky those who were south of the Gothic Line, where the Allies were in charge. They had food and slept peacefully, but north of the front looting and robberies were the order of the day, and you just went hungry.

Maria decided to salvage what she could. She moved her best furniture to Cà degli Alessandri, a little farm away from the village. She had the white and blue Ginori crockery, together with a couple of small paintings and other valuable objects, walled up in the stable. Then she had a pile of wood and several bundles of sticks heaped against the wall to disguise the wet cement.

29th September, 1944, Covigliajo, near the Futa Pass, between Bologna and Florence.

"I can't take much more of this fucking weather!" It had been raining for two days, and by now Stephen was in a foul mood. Around him there was only mud. It seemed that the mountains were melting. Partly because of the rain, partly because Germans blew them up, roads were full of craters. The day before a soldier had fallen into the mud up to his armpits.

"When I go home to Texas, I will never camp again in my life!"

"I do not know where to dry the stuff."

"The other morning when we woke up there was even fog inside the tent."

"Why had we to end up in this shit hole of a place I don't know! When I think of the girls we left in Florence..."

"Hey, do you still have razor blades?"

Stephen threw them to him on the cot and kept shaving. *Bloody Germans!* The front was a little farther on, beyond Pietramala. Soon they would be there.

"Do you know that guy Jim and the others, last night, oops... the wind blew down their tent! I bet this morning they're not in such a good mood..."

They climbed into the Jeep. The evening before, it had taken Stephen an hour to remove the mud from the wheels and the body of the car.

"Come on, today we'll put our boots up the Jerries' arses!"

They arrived at Pietramala around noon. The road was a nightmare and then they were blocked. They continued on foot, with the guns on their shoulders, towards the Raticosa Pass. There was dense fog. You could not see a hundred feet. And the wind was so strong that when a soldier shouted something to Stephen he only saw his lips move. Danger could lurk everywhere and no one wanted to be a dead hero.

You could understand immediately that you were at the front. The Germans had run away so fast that next to the pass there was still an ambulance. On the ground beside it, a couple of dead Germans.

Stephen found himself thinking that the day before at that time they were still alive.

At the pass, the fog was even thicker despite the increasing gusts of wind. Awful weather.

The signs of the fighting were everywhere: broken trees, telephone poles that lay on the ground.

The bodies of two other Germans stuck out from a hole at the side of the road. Those dead men were the price to pay. Beyond the Raticosa Pass the road ran down towards the great Po valley. They had to get out of those mountains. They had to liberate the country, to give hope back to the people.

But the Germans could open fire at any time. There could be snipers hidden in the fog.

A shot was heard and another, and then excited voices. He saw a man advancing with his hands raised. Two of Stephen's comrades took him to the lieutenant to be questioned.

No trace of his brothers.

Stephen stopped to smoke a cigarette. From time to time the wind blew the low clouds away just enough to show a stretch of meadow or a mountain top. Then greyness reigned again.

That curtain of thick fog gave them a sense of security.

A Jeep reached them: "Guys! The order is to advance to the next village: La Posta. You have to search all the houses. You'll stay there for the night."

"At least we're not sleeping in a tent. Last night it rained on my head. I had to sleep with my helmet on."

The road began to descend. From a distance came the sound of explosions. The Germans were beyond Filigare. Around a bend, here was La Posta. There was not a soul in that little hamlet. After exploring one of the poor houses from top to bottom, Stephen and his companions settled there.

"We can even make a fire because with this fog the Jerries won't see the smoke!"

"Yes, but where's the firewood?"

"You have it under your eyes... Let's burn the table and chairs and sit on the floor in front of the fireplace. I found a blanket to spread so that your ass doesn't get cold."

They began to smash the furniture.

"Guys, it's amazing! In the chicken coop behind the house there are two chickens, and they've also laid eggs!"

"I can already smell roast chickens! Don't tell the others, otherwise we'll have to share them. Ain't we been lucky?"

5th October 1944, Loiano.

The men of the 362nd Regiment had liberated Monghidoro on 2nd October, but the clashes continued mile after mile. On 5th October the American troops arrived in Loiano. To take the village, they lined up eight tanks.

When the first two tanks approached the houses they were hit and caught fire. While the teams came out of the vehicles, a grenade cut a soldier in half.

The tanks burned long. The operation had failed. The infantry postponed the attack, and the initiative passed to the artillery, which fired more than four thousand shots on Loiano. The village was destroyed. Not only the houses, but even the trees clinging to the mountain were in pieces.

When night fell, the tanks continued to burn. From a distance, the Americans saw the Germans move in the light of the flames.

The gunfire resumed the morning after. Another morning of fog and rain. The displaced villagers heard the shots from afar. They had found refuge in farms or in the caves that peasants had dug in the sandy soil.

At one point the shots ceased. The infantry ventured through the rubble. A fight from house to house began. Among the gunfire, music could be heard: a woman's voice, lazy and sensual, sang in German. A radio was playing in the middle of the ruins. Perhaps to say that Loiano was Germany.

An American soldier, lurking behind a wall, saw the radio and fired. Then it was silence, but it lasted only an instant. The shots and screams resumed. Orders given in German or English. The noise of the rubble on which soldiers ran for cover. The scream of a man who had been hit. A wall that collapsed after a machine gun barrage was unleashed.

Then it was really silent, while the Americans patrolled the ruins, looking for snipers, but there were no more Germans.

The problem at that point was the burned trucks, which hindered their passage. In the course of the day they were removed and the road to Sabbioni was cleared of mines. The Americans had to dump truckloads of rubble where the craters prevented vehicles from advancing. And they had to take care of the prisoners, the dead and the wounded on both sides. There was lots of work for everyone, but soon it was dark.

6th October 1944, Loiano.

The next morning, Stephen and Jim drove on a Jeep through what was left of Loiano. The village was devastated. The bell tower was full of holes. "Christ," said Jim. When they stopped in the square, they were approached by two children in rags. The Americans had some sweets, which they threw to them.

An old woman was sitting on a heap of ruins. She was not crying. She was just sitting, with her black dress and headscarf, her chin resting on her arm. What was she looking at? Perhaps at some scene from the past, at the village as it used to be, as she wanted to remember it. Perhaps she was just unable to think.

Stephen could still hear the explosions that had rocked the mountains. That noise which had seemed endless now lay down with the dust.

He lit a cigarette.

A lame man drew up a cart alongside a house that had been half destroyed. A woman carried out everyday objects one by one. Aligned on the road there were two chairs, a coffee grinder, kitchen utensils of which he did not know the use, a white enamel bowl. The man went into the house and came out with a table on his head. He put it on the cart with its legs in the air. The woman followed with the drawer.

Men were moving among the ruins like ants. Ants in the sand, ants in the rocks. *We're just insects*, thought Stephen, still smoking.

He heard a column of tanks approach on that road that was full of holes and mud, even in the centre of the village. *More insects.* Hard-shelled, like cockroaches. When you crush them they crack.

War was like that. It took off the frame that surrounded human beings, the frame of your social position, the frame of habits, the frame of conventions. What remained was the animal part. Insects buzzing in the sky. Insects on mounds of sand. Insects in a row, like those hairy caterpillars that nest on pine trees and form a column when they move.

Here he was again, still comparing everything to insects.

As a child he had been afraid of caterpillars. Until one day he had taken a stick and knelt down. At the touch of the stick, the caterpillars had curled up, like so many rings, one after the other. A moment later, Stephen was running home crying. His father had put his hand under cold water. He had explained that caterpillars sprayed a stinging liquid. A form of defence.

It was a law of nature: attack and defence. It all came down to that if you took off the frame. Fail or prevail. They had to win the war!

Stephen began to wander among the ruins. In a side street he saw an abandoned truck. "Hey, Jim, come on! It's not in bad condition. A real stroke of luck, eh!"

"Let's tow it to the repair unit and put it back on the road. Just what we need, right?"

7th October 1944, Loiano.

Her precautions had worked. At least they had not found the objects she had walled in the stable, but they had taken away what they could anyway. Not to mention what was left under the rubble. Maria began to write, as she had been advised, the *List of movable property belonging to the Sig.ra Maria Galli, widow Ascari, removed by German troops on 29th September, 1944*:

1 – A five valve radio, unbranded.

2 – A large oil painting, 2.50 x 1.50m., sacred subject depicting "The visit of S. Elizabeth" by an unknown artist, presumably sixteenth century.

3 – An oil painting, 2 x 1.30m., sacred subject depicting "The Annunciation" by an unknown artist, presumably sixteenth century.

4 – An oil painting, 1.80 x 1.30m., depicting the Virgin and Child, also by an unknown artist, date unknown.

5 – An oval painting depicting St. Anthony of Padua with rich antique gold frame. Both the picture and the frame date presumably from the seventeenth century. Artist unknown.

6 – No. 10 hens

7 – No. 2 geese, weighing five kilos each

8 – 5.5 tons of seasoned hay

9 – 2.4 tons of straw

10 – 2 tons of dry wood for burning

11 – No. 100 bundles of dry firewood

12 – 8 light bulbs

13 – 8 glass dishes

That was all. Maria thought of the beautiful paintings that were no longer there, but she had good reasons not to complain. It was enough to look at the village, at the way it had been reduced. Poor people! And her sister's house, next door. There was nothing left to save. At least she had a roof over her head, although part of the house had fallen down.

She thought that worse things had recently happened. Much worse.

By now rumour had spread of the massacres that the Nazis had carried out on the 29th a few valleys away, around Marzabotto. Could they have gone so far? *God! God!* Maria began to pray for all those who were gone, for all the mothers whose children were dead.

She thought of her children. Giulio was a prisoner of the Allies in Africa. She knew nothing could happen to him. But Antonio? The image of her son, alone up there in Germany, among a foreign and enemy people, leapt forward with all the intensity of feeling and squeezed her heart.

With a wave of anger she threw away the list she had written from the table and she began to cry with her head in her hands.

14th October 1944, Travesio.

The news had been spreading for days: *Here come the Cossacks!* They had already seen so much. Was it possible that this would also happen on top of all the rest? And what did it mean? *They will take our homes, they will take our things. They will come to live here!* Were the Nazis really going to give Friuli to those nomad people? Why?

When the Germans invaded the Soviet Union, the Cossacks – who were loyal to the Tsar and opposed to the Stalin regime – had passed to the enemy. Following the withdrawal of their allies, the Cossacks had moved to Ukraine and Poland, where they had helped the Nazis suppress the Warsaw uprising.

Between late July and early August, more than twenty thousand Cossacks and a few thousand Caucasians had arrived in Friuli on military trains. They had camped in the areas of Amaro, Osoppo and Gemona, but the Nazis intended to transfer them to the mountains, where the partisans' resistance was harder to eradicate. *Operation Ataman* would turn Carnia into a new *Kosakenland*!

For days the people of Travesio listened with awe to the tales of those who had seen the nomad people. Then it happened. Two little boys crossed the square on their bikes, shouting: "Here come the Cossacks! Here come the Cossacks!"

Bepi took Amalia by her arm. While he quickly closed the shutters of the café, she went upstairs to look for their daughters. Thank God they were at home!

Then they heard the sound of a horn. People looked out of the windows. Even Ester and Delia could not resist the temptation to stand behind the curtains, their eyes wide open.

At the head of the caravan there were men on horseback. While crossing the village they shouted. Someone even fired a shot into the air. They wore big fur hats and had cartridge belts intertwined on their chest. They carried swords and daggers.

Their families followed. Women and children, bent old ladies, patriarchs with hollow faces and long beards, all crammed into shabby wagons, loaded with pots, demijohns, wooden boxes and bags of food, piles of carpets, blankets, animal skins.

Behind each family wagon came the animals: horses, cows, sheep, goats. Even a camel! The animals were emaciated. The humans were dirty and tired. When they passed by, the smell of the moving tribe seeped into the houses.

It took a good quarter of an hour before the caravan had gone. Amalia was shuttling between the café and the first floor. She did not want to leave her husband alone, but she was terrified at the idea that somebody might notice her daughters at the window.

Her heart calmed down only when outside everything was silence.

The Cossacks were gone, but their smell still hovered, together with their tenacity.

Towards evening they learned that some of those Cossacks had stopped in Clauzetto, up in the mountains. The local people had been forced to house them. Some of the villagers had been driven out of their homes.

Amalia made the sign of the cross. Would this war never be over?

20th October 1944, Travesio.

"I don't like sleeping here. I've taken a room in Usago, where you are more relaxed, where there is no danger." Amalia could not take it any more. Every night she kept waiting, without sleeping: waiting for a shot, a cry, the sound of tyres.

Sleeping in the square was not safe. Better to leave the village. Bepi and Ennio would remain to watch the house. Amalia wanted Delia and Ester with her.

Two nights went by. Amalia had caught up on her sleep. By day they went back to the village and opened the café. Those were bad times. You never knew what could happen. In the morning, she stopped at the church to pray with her daughters. In the evening she was in a hurry to get to Usago. All three of them were cycling.

That morning, Amalia gave a start. She felt she had heard a noise. The slightest thing woke her up. She stood for a moment with her senses alert. Crack! This time she could not have dreamed of it. Crack! A pebble against the window.

Amalia got out of bed. She looked at the clock. *Not yet five! My God! My God!* Her legs were shaking. Turning the handle of the window and opening the shutters took all the strength she had at her disposal. Outside it was dark.

"We're looking for the schoolmistress. We're looking for the Signorina."

She had already understood. She did not even have the strength to ask who was looking for her daughter at that time. Ester had heard too. She walked over to the window. She would be downstairs in a moment. She began to dress, without looking at anyone, without thinking. Delia felt tears well up in her eyes, but she could not cry.

Lord, help us! Lord, please. Amalia was a mother. Her every thought, her every sense was focused on the daughter they were taking away from her.

Ester embraced her mother without speaking. Delia kept swallowing her sobs. Nobody understood anything. As if everything was spinning round and round and round. The door opened. Ester was gone.

Delia threw herself on the bed and started crying. "Mum, Mum!" She ran to the feet of her mother, who was sitting in a corner, her hand resting on the windowsill. She was crying on the lap of her mother, lifeless, but the heat of her daughter gave life back to her. "Let's go home!"

Meanwhile, Ester, on her bike, was crossing the dark streets of the village. She was escorted by two young men.

Once they reached the next village, she was asked to leave her bicycle. "We'll continue on foot." Ester wore shoes with heels. They began to climb a dirt road in the mountains.

At times, Ester's head was full of things. *Mum. Dad. They will be afraid.* It was too late to comfort them. Perhaps she would not see them any more. The next moment she had no thoughts. Only pain in her feet, cold on her shoulders. Only silence and fear.

The sun was rising. A late autumn dawn. Leaves had fallen in the woods. The dewy air already felt like winter.

They arrived at a village in the mountains. The partisans went into a house and left her outside, sitting on the wet grass.

When she was alone she burst into tears. She knew the family who lived opposite. She saw a fleeting face behind a window. No one talked to her.

The partisans came out. The group began to climb again. *I know them, I know them,* she thought. Did this mean salvation or damnation?

20th October 1944, unknown place.

It was late morning when they reached the place. The first sign was a whistle. A whistle in response. A clearing. A house. A barn.

There were fifteen, perhaps twenty men up there. Men with guns. The war was closer than she had ever seen it. So close that it could stretch its indifferent fingers towards her and crush her.

They gave her a piece of bread with cheese. They poured water into a glass that was stained with red wine. She drank and ate. Then they sat her on the straw in the stable, under the barn, and the waiting began. She watched the light come through the door. Time felt unreal.

Suddenly, Ester heard a voice: "Tell me where she is."

"Dad!" Even as the word came up to her mouth, she found herself standing. She saw her father pass by and he saw her in turn. She experienced the joy of meeting his eyes, the pain of losing him, while a partisan led him beyond, the anxiety of uncertainty. Ester ran to the door. Her father was made to climb a ladder, which was taken away.

He was in the barn above her! At the back of the building there was a small window with bars. Ester approached it. "Dad," she whispered. "Dad!" she called again.

"Ester! Are you okay?"

"What happened?"

"They came home. They took me away along with Ennio. Then they let Ennio go. Speak softly, otherwise they'll hear us."

Everything was different. Her father was with her. But inside her it all suddenly clouded up. What if her father had not gone back? Ester dropped onto the straw. She had no spark of energy left. Fatigue bordered on the irrepressible need to know. What did they want to do to her? What had she done?

At last, they called her. She limped to the house on her broken heels. Beside the fireplace was a table. Two men were sitting behind it.

One of them was called Ettore and loved books by Dostoyevsky.

Ester waited. "She's the GIL Inspector of Travesio," said a partisan who was standing against the window. Nobody asked Ester to sit.

"We know you are a member of the Social Republic!"

Ester fell from the clouds. "It's not true!"

"We found your card!"

She summoned the strength to fight back. "It's not possible! I haven't ever had it. I've nothing to do with the *Repubblica Sociale!*"

Silence.

"You remember," said one of the men seated at the table, "the day of the attack on the Workers' Society." Ester nodded.

"Where were you on that day?"

"In the morning I went to teach in Toppo, then I came home. In the afternoon I was at home."

"Somebody saw you, after the attack, on the premises of the Society."

"It's true. I went to see what remained of the drawing school, like everybody else. The whole village was there."

"You made a gesture that we do not like."

"What gesture? What are you talking about?"

"You tore up a red handkerchief that you found in the table drawer!"

Ester had never seen any red handkerchief, but faced with the unexpectedness of that accusation she felt the need to delve into her memory. After a moment, she regained her foothold. "It's not true. I haven't torn any handkerchief!" She wanted to ask them who had come up with such an idea, but she could not. She knew that they would not answer. It was not she who was putting questions.

"Somebody saw you!"

Who could that be? Who might want to harm her? Resisting the temptation of losing herself in that thought, she found the strength to say the right thing: "I was not alone. There was Flavia with me. Ask her! Ask her if you do not believe me!"

"Flavia who?" asked the man who was standing.

"Flavia Bedosti. We entered together. We also went out together."

"For the time that's enough," said Ettore, who until then had not opened his mouth. He could not understand that strange girl. Had he been able to ask her what books she read, he would have got a clearer idea of her. But perhaps she just did not read. And then that was not the kind of question you could ask in such a situation.

They took her back to the stable. She exchanged a few words with her father. She told him what the charges were. He comforted her. If that was the reason why they had taken them, it would be all cleared up. It was just a mistake.

That night they did not give her anything to eat, but she was not hungry. Her eyes were closing through emotion and fatigue. Her legs felt heavy. She took off her shoes. Her blisters ached. She curled up on the straw. She pressed her clothes and coat against her. The voices were so far away. She did not have time to stop her thoughts before she fell asleep.

An animal! An animal that was crawling on her. It crawled on her side. Now it was wet, there on her neck.

In a flash she was awake. She felt the man lying beside her, on her, looking for her with his tongue and his hands. His breath smelled of wine.

She wanted to shout, but her voice failed her.

Her arms rejected the mouth that was looking for her, the breath that was soiling her. She fought with all her strength, while the man weighed on her, pushing on her. While the man was wearing down her resistance with his desire.

At last, a cry escaped her previously paralysed muscles, which were now out of control. But already a heavy hand was choking her. With a spasm, her teeth closed on that hand. Through the ceiling, she could already hear her father shouting: "Ester! Ester!"

The slimy animal broke away from her. She did not see his face, but she knew his smell. He pulled away from her and walked out of the door in silence. She saw a dark shape bring his hand to his mouth.

Her father was still calling from above, his voice broken: "Ester! Speak to me!"

She found the strength to respond: "Don't be afraid, Dad. I'm alone. I love you Dad!"

Ester fell back to the ground, under the little window. If she was to die the next day, she could well spend the night awake. She began to pray nervously. The cold and hunger did the rest.

21st October 1944, unknown place.

The next day there was fog. She saw it from the very first. The cold was more intense. She tried to pull herself to her feet. They hurt. She began to tremble.

"Come with me," said a voice from the door. They took her into the house. In the kitchen, a fire burned in the fireplace. They gave her a bowl of milk with bread in it. She ate greedily. They looked at her. She thanked them and stood up. She wrapped her coat tight and started back to the stable.

No one followed her. They let her go as someone who is at home. Then she heard her father come down from the barn. There was something to eat for him too. In her heart, she thanked them for this. Poor Dad. He had ended up there because of her!

The morning was spent in silence. Bepi asked her how she felt. She replied that everything was fine. They had nothing to say. Each spared words and thoughts, as if to escape the black core at the heart of their future.

At lunchtime, no one showed up. The afternoon began to flow. Hoarse voices. People coming and going. And the strange sense of being already beyond life, in a land that was in between. The idea of dying! What a strange end. Disappearing like that, young as she was, full of life, without having found love. But war and fate had no pity.

She thought of her mother and Delia and Ennio, who the day before had returned home. At least he was there with them. At least they were not alone. It was all her fault! But what had she done? So deep was her bewilderment, when she thought of her accusation, that she wondered if she really had snatched the handkerchief, if that act had not slipped from her memory.

The day passed like that, in a valley of visions that bordered on delirium. When inner mists finally turned into unconsciousness, she felt snakes slip into her clothes and she was shaken by spasms. Her mind was still fighting shadows when a man woke her up, handing her something to eat. She had slept all afternoon. Now she could watch through the night, in the hazy darkness of that place without contours.

22nd October 1944, unknown place.

When morning came she was asleep against the wall. She woke up with a start. She had a stiff neck. She was cold and hungry and tired, but the thing she wanted most was to know her fate, if it was time to live or die. The sun was high when they called her. She entered the room. She faced those men.

They had talked with Flavia. The charge had been dropped.

In the courtyard her father was waiting. They hugged. Then they silently followed the men who would take them back to their normal lives. They abandoned the misty mountain limbo, unable to believe it was all over. They walked away, step by step, from those nights and those days of fear, from the maze of dark thoughts.

They found the road leading down the mountain. They crossed the first villages. In front of the house of a girl she knew, Ester saw her bicycle. She did not go and get it. She kept silent, her hand tightly in her father's, until they reached the village square.

When Amalia saw them it was as if a coat of lead had fallen from her shoulders, as if she had come back to life with them. Ester ran to meet her. They hugged, and never wanted to let go of each other. The warmth of her daughter's body melted the frost of her unbearable waiting. Tears mingled with tears.

Bepi reached the two women. He pressed their heads to his chest with tender strength. Meanwhile, his eyes too swelled with tears. And he thought how happy he was to be a father, how beautiful life was.

Although it would be over one day, no one was going to take that time from him. That moment was his forever to cherish in the innermost part of his heart. He had been able to bring his daughter home. God had not deprived him of that good and brave and beautiful girl, who was so headstrong and stupid at times, that girl he had been given as a gift so he could take care of her.

His family was reunited.

13th November 1944, Werneuchen.

That was a bad time. There was less and less to eat. And a fellow prisoner had suffered an exemplary punishment. He had picked from the rubble of a bombed building a comb, a razor, some razor blades, a jar of plums in brandy. The police had found the items while they searched the camp. He had been arrested and a Special Court had sentenced him to death. At the last moment they had commuted the sentence to ten years in prison.

He got up, like everyone else, when it was still dark and began to shave. Perhaps because he had just woken up, perhaps because of something he had dreamed of that night, he found himself thinking about the Albergo Pellegrino. He was in his room, preparing to go down. It was summer. At his age he was growing a belly.

With an effort he tore himself from those thoughts which at first did him good, but then hurt.

He had been allotted a strange life. When had it happened? Where was the fork in the road that had brought him there? Had he stayed in Loiano, perhaps at that time he would have woken up with Elsa at his side. He still loved her, even though he loved Pina. Sometimes he thought of her with tenderness. But that was no longer his life. Had he been allowed to go back, he would not have changed anything.

They would not take his life away from him. He had to accept everything. In the name of the persons he loved, of the past that had made him what he was.

22nd December 1944, Werneuchen.

What a Christmas was in store! After working for twelve hours they went back to the huts so tired that they longed only to sleep. When would it be over? He prayed to God that he would let him go home in the end. He thought of Pina.

When he shut his eyes, before falling asleep, he heard the music of her piano coming from the next room. She had taught him to love music, although he had never understood it. He had a good ear, she said.

In those cold nights, with no warmth and no food, he fed on the notes that memory brought to that brick barracks from another place and another time. He listened to the pieces that his wife used to play.

There was a prelude that she had taught him to love. "It's called *The Raindrop*," she had told him on a distant day. "Chopin wrote this while he was ill and lived in Majorca. George Sand had gone somewhere. Chopin started playing. The notes mingled with the rain."

Antonio was smiling. He liked it when Pina told him a story and put all her passion into it.

"In that solitude, Chopin had a vision, perhaps a dream. He was dead and a raindrop kept falling on his chest. But as he woke after dying, after feeling he had died, this melody sprang from his heart. He thought it was a foreboding. He thought that George Sand had had an accident; that she had died. He was desperate. Then she came back and they embraced."

Antonio's smile had widened. Pina jumped off her chair and ran to the piano.

"I know it is a strange story, but if you listen to the prelude you will understand everything. You have to listen to the raindrop falling. It's sad, but it's so beautiful."

Pina's hands had moved. And through that music a raindrop was guiding him. The same note repeated over and over again, with the insistence of a rainy day. As if that drop contained an entire life, with all its joy, its suffering, everything a human being can feel.

In that brick barracks that was covered with snow, in the north without hope, he listened once more to the music she used to play. He saw himself as a child, seated on a small wicker loveseat by the window. Next to him a grey-green cat. He had not thought of this in years. Outside the window drops kept falling. All the same and yet all different. Drops in which he saw all his life reflected. Each of us like a raindrop. Each of us subject to the whim of a rainy day.

He felt a tear fall. Yet another drop. No more than a drop. Can you love a tear drop? At that time, for him, that drop was her. She was getting to him through those sounds. She would never leave him alone for she was inside him.

He turned towards the wall, warm with a happiness he had not known in months. I have had my Christmas gift, he thought, surrendering to the call of unconsciousness which welcomed him every night, that inanimate night he now loved much more than daylight.

An instant later a fellow prisoner called him to ask for a cigarette: "Antonio, psst! No way: he's already sleeping... Lucky him!"

3rd April 1945, Werneuchen.

Death was in the air. The great Germany was agonising and the Nazis wanted to drag down with them all those who had contributed to its decline. Life in the camp was becoming harder every day. Sudden roll calls, backpack inspections, even propaganda lessons, everyone standing outdoors.

At night the bombings prevented them from sleeping. There were continuous alarms. They went to bed fully clothed, ready to get up suddenly and run to shelters. And when they returned to the barracks it was already morning. They lay half an hour on their bunks to get up with a headache and a whole day before them, without even knowing where they would be taken.

During the last two weeks, instead of sending them to factories, the Germans loaded them onto trucks. You could spend all day shovelling rubble, pulling out dead bodies. Or digging anti-tank defences, under pouring rain and even snow. Blisters and chilblains were added to hunger and cold.

Back at the camp, when you were lucky, you found a few potatoes in the broth. The little rye bread was increasingly black and stringy. If you were not careful, someone stole it from under your nose, as happened one day to Antonio. He could not believe it.

Yet, the opposite might also happen. One of the men from his barracks found a pile of potato skins that somebody had thrown in the garbage. They roasted them and ate them together. It was a party.

Antonio had seen his companions weaken. Some of them, when they could, leaned on a cane while walking. Then they began to disappear, one after the other. A fever or dysentery sufficed. If you could not get up, if you could not pretend that everything was back to normal, you were taken away. And you did not come back.

They lived like that, clinging to life tooth and nail, asking for God's help, cursing the Germans.

Bologna Polonia

21st April 1945, Bologna.

The city was deserted in that Saturday dawn as the soldiers of the Second Polish Corps approached the centre. Those men were advancing cautiously, rifles in hand, for fear of ambushes. Was it possible that the Germans had gone just like that?

As they advanced in that suspended atmosphere, in that ghost town, Father Grzondiel prayed and thought. He did not know where thought ended and prayer began. When you are a military chaplain you learn not to go in for subtlety.

"If God exists," he said at times from the altar, "He's certainly not an accountant! But the more generous He is, the more we are called to be generous!" And he thundered those words because he could not stand the drip-feeding of Christianity.

As in love. Even if he had never had a woman, he knew what it meant to love. Giving all of oneself, never computing. No, God was not a book-keeper. Otherwise he would never have sacrificed His son for a bunch of misfits like us.

Along the way there were many buildings in ruins. The Bolognese had removed just enough rubble to pass through but next to the pavement there were piles of bricks and mortar and beams.

How different this place was from his native Poland. And he had seen so many places in those years. He travelled with his mind. He went back to '39, when he was chaplain of the military hospital of Zbaraz, and the Bolsheviks took him prisoner. *Kampania wrześniowa.* The September campaign. The partition of Poland. *My God, my God: help me not to feel hatred!* He found himself praying as he felt his teeth clench.

That had marked the beginning of his exodus. First Budapest and then Athens, where he had become chaplain at the embassy. Who would have thought, when he taught literature in Poznan, that he would have ended up in Beirut, in Damascus, in Baghdad? And in December '43 in Italy with the Second Polish Corps!

Italy. The Pope. God had been generous with him. For others, war was only a succession of suffering. For him it was experience. He had known people and countries. He had learned to take leave – from his land, from his habits.

As taught by St. Francis, he did not care about tomorrow. He lived like the flowers of the field and the birds in heaven, trusting in God's mercy. He wanted to be an instrument of His Providence, to second His designs. Easy to say...

They had entered the old town. Here were the famous arcades of which he had heard. And the beautiful buildings.

Behind the windows, people stared at the roaring tanks, at the soldiers who marched in the street. They were still afraid. He could feel it in the air. They were right. There was the danger of snipers, of stragglers, the danger of some bloodthirsty madman who was determined not to lose his personal battle.

Father Giovanni – as he was known by many, or even as Don Giovanni, no less than Don Juan, since Jan was his middle name – found himself praying. He prayed so that a morning of joy would not become a morning of blood, so that people would breathe again the air of freedom.

Here were the Leaning Towers. He had heard so much about them! But soldiers had to keep their eyes open. Anything could happen.

On the way, two men in civilian clothes came towards them with raised arms. An officer came up to Father Giovanni, who spoke good Italian, asking him to act as an interpreter.

One of the two civilians lowered his arms and held out his hand: "Welcome to Bologna! We were expecting you. The Germans are gone. The partisans are already in control of the main public buildings. The Liberation Committee has appointed me as mayor. My name is Giuseppe Dozza."

"I am... military chaplain Jan, Giovanni Grzondiel," said the priest with a northern accent, "I'll translate what you have said."

The officers in charge of the Poles did not know whether to trust this man, and advanced cautiously towards Piazza Maggiore. From the side streets the first of the curious approached. The tension was palpable. The Poles looked in front, sideways, behind. Anything could happen at any time.

When they entered Piazza Maggiore, a soldier saw something move in the shade of the arcades. He fired. There was a hail of shots. Then there was silence.

Signor Dozza returned with a group of civilians.

"This is Antonio Zoccoli, the regional president of the National Liberation Committee," he told Father Giovanni. "The city is free. There is no reason to be afraid. There are no Germans here! Our men have gone to seek the former *Podestà* for the transfer of power."

They talked in the middle of the square, then they joined the *Podestà* in the Town Hall. It was at that point that Dozza and Zoccoli made the proposal: "Father Giovanni, since it is you Poles who have freed Bologna, today we would like to see your flag waving from the Asinelli Tower. It is the highest in the city!"

As he climbed the narrow wooden staircase with the flag in his hand, Father Giovanni felt he was experiencing a solemn moment. They went out on the terrace on top of the tower. It dominated the whole of Bologna. Entering the city he had not noticed that the hills were so close.

Suddenly the bells started ringing. He heard the joyful cries of the people in the streets – in the long street that stretched like a carpet at his feet. And when his hands hoisted the flag of his country, of his battered and hurt Poland, his body began to tremble. His hands were steady, but his body was shaking. Even his teeth chattered and there was nothing he could do to control himself. All his will was concentrated in those hands, consigned to the task, indeed the honour, to tighten the straps, while already the white and red of Poland was waving in the morning air.

He felt the sky smiling above that city, regaining peace. He felt that between the city and his country there was a special bond. Ever since he had read for the first time the name of that place, which his northern pronunciation made so close to the Italian name of his homeland: *Bologna Polonia*. On top of that tower he felt at home. And the wind of his land filled his heart.

21st April 1945, Werneuchen.

Since the dawn of the 16th Berlin had been under Soviet attack. Constant fire from the ground and from the sky: pieces of artillery, Katyusha rockets, Sturmovik bombers. The airspace above the city was traversed by the beams of hundreds of reflectors.

In Werneuchen, which is a few miles from Berlin, the night was filled with smoke and flame, while the relentless roar sounded like the trumpets of judgement. The war spoke to the camp prisoners with its strange language. Promises of freedom and death threats.

That morning, when it was time to gather for the roll call, the prisoners realised that something was happening. "Everybody out with their backpacks," said the barracks chief.

Once they were grouped in the large open space in front of the guards' tower, they were divided into groups. The loudspeaker recited those words clearly: "Evacuation of the field." Antonio and his companions saw the first group march towards the exit. Their turn came. But where would they take them?

With their backpacks on their shoulders, they almost could not stand up. Not to mention walk. They wore half-broken or mismatched shoes, even wooden clogs. Their feet were swaddled in rags. They advanced swaying like animals along a road that led north, while military vehicles sped past.

A man, one of the first in line, fell down. Due to the weight of the backpack he rolled into the ditch beside the road. A guard approached. Antonio saw the man's face contort, then heard his cry: "*Nein, nein! Bitte!*" A gunshot put an end to it.

The man in front of Antonio had his hand splashed with blood. He clutched it instinctively and made a gesture as if to wipe it on his trousers, then he did not. Antonio understood.

They turned right onto a smaller road, a dirt road. After hours of walking they let them sit next to a fountain. They were allowed to drink, one at a time. Back on their feet. The march resumed. It lasted all day.

It was almost dark when they arrived in a village. There was no one. Civilians had all fled. In the distance you could hear bursts, explosions. The guards locked them up in the school. They were alone, without food but alone. How long would it last? How long would it take to die? Antonio was ready to go. He had struggled to stay attached to life, but everything has a limit. Every life has a limit. Why not leave now?

During the night they could still hear bombs falling. Antonio hoped that a bomb would hit them. He wanted to leave like that, along with his companions. They had shared hell. They could well share freedom. What was waiting for them was certainly a better world. And if there was nothing it mattered little.

Putting an end to life, *not being* was already enough. When you suffer you learn to content yourself.

22nd April 1945, unknown place.

The next morning no one came to wake them up. When Antonio opened his eyes the sun was already high. Someone exclaimed: "Hey, they've left us here. They've gone away like that." They opened the windows on the ground floor, threw the backpacks to the ground and hoisted themselves down. The stronger helped the weak.

They were free, but free to do what?

Antonio looked at his companions. They were all gaunt. In a year he had lost nearly two stone. And that cough that shook him...

The first thing was looking for something to eat. They found turnips, a few potatoes, black bread. They ate voraciously and angrily, but they soon stopped. You had to save that food, to think about tomorrow.

The Italians held a meeting. Getting back to Italy crossing Germany was to be excluded. They would meet only enemies. Yet, they had to get away from Berlin. Hell was there. The resistance of the Germans would last until the end.

The closest country was Poland and they headed east. Thus began a journey in which hope and despair swapped roles a hundred times each day. They slept in barns and abandoned houses, sometimes in the open. They picked their food in overgrown kitchen gardens, from cellars they broke into, hoping to find something they could put in their mouths.

The seven Italians shared everything. They worked as a team. Solidarity and homesickness were the only forces that drove them to fight.

In a house they had found a pistol. They were ready to go to any extreme.

24th April 1945, Kostrzyn, Poland.

At the end of three days they crossed the Oder river and reached the town of Kostrzyn. The town was in rubble. A Catholic priest put them up and gave them food. To make sure no one would hurt them, he lodged them in the church, locking them in.

They fell asleep at five in the afternoon. Antonio woke up in the middle of the night to answer the call of nature. They had put a bucket in a corner thinking of that. They would empty it the next morning.

The church was dark, but the moon shone through the high windows. In that blue light, statues and stuccoes came to life. They seemed to caress him. After facing so much horror, he found again the beautiful and the good. In the darkness of the night he had risked not knowing, the moon was there to show him the lining of the world.

He did not even think of his wife or his mother, of the breath-taking beauty of his homeland. He was serene, simply serene. Despite everything he had gone through, they had not succeeded in wielding the greatest evil, the ultimate evil. He was there with his companions. A brother among brothers.

He had dozed off many times in churches, as a child and even growing up. Instead, that night... he had never been so alert, so attentive. He had never felt so in touch with the outside world, as if a thousand threads started from his body, a thousand branches that spread towards that universe from which for an entire year he had felt excluded.

He thought back to the brick barracks where he had spent nearly four hundred nights. He thought back to the miserable backyards and to the miserable meadows that surrounded the barracks, and to the barbed wire that enclosed that miserable corner of a miserable world. He had come out of that cage, and only now did he understand – did he know for sure – that beneath the thin shell of his skin and bones something had never died. They had not got to his soul.

He took a few steps and he bathed in the moonlight. He saw his shadow on the floor. He held out his hand in the clean air, as if to touch it. He watched his hand disappear and reappear in that hospitable space.

He went to pee in the corner of the church where they had placed the bucket and felt that in such a humble and human gesture Christ was close to him.

I would like to know what happened when the priest of Kostrzyn church opened the bolt and released the seven Italians from that holy prison. I would like to know what happened in the following days, and how our heroes covered the four hundred miles that separate Kostrzyn from Lublin.

I would like to interrogate Antonio in his sleep. He is still asleep, exhausted by fatigue, even after the priest entered the church and began to speak Latin with one of Antonio's fellows, a fellow who has studied at the grammar school. I walk over to Antonio. I try to touch his shoulder, to whisper in his ear, saying: "It's me. You can tell me everything," but he keeps sleeping. He has other things to think about. Perhaps he does not want to think.

I just have to leave Antonio to his fate, knowing that in a few days I will find him in Lublin. Yes, because that is where Antonio has an appointment.

1st May 1945, Travesio.

"You came to dance too... But aren't you afraid of your mother?" These words were addressed to Ester as she entered the Workers' Society hall, wholly decorated to celebrate the liberation of Italy from fascism. Going to that party might mean meeting people that Ester would not have wanted to meet, but it also meant putting an end to what had happened to her.

"You're beautiful, Ester," said a girl who came from Trieste, laying a hand on her shoulder and making her turn. Ester had a shimmering dress, a dark grey ground with scarlet highlights.

"Will you dance with me tonight?" asked a young man.

Somebody offered her a glass of white wine. She did not want to take it, then she accepted it.

There were lights and voices, and the music soon began. Her knight came to claim her. Ester put down her glass. She had barely touched it.

Suddenly she saw the face of the young man darken. She turned towards the door. Standing between two wings of people there was her mother, wearing her black apron. Amalia reached out, gripped her hair and dragged her away without saying a word.

Ester came down the stairs in silence, tears streaming down her face. A hand like a claw held her by the hair, but her mother did not even look at her.

When they were in the backyard and the music was distant, Amalia said: "You have a boyfriend. Do you think that Giulio would be happy?"

Ester began to sob. She wanted to tell her: *I didn't go just for me. I did it for you. I was scared!* But no words came to the surface. The water was dense and opaque.

So Ester just ran to her room, locking the door and throwing herself on the bed, fully dressed as she was.

She remembered a time, years before, when she was still a child. She was reading a book in her room.

"What is it you're reading?" asked her mother.

"A book."

"What's the title?"

"*Happiness Is Simple*," said Ester, and she realised that her mother did not like the title.

"Let me see it!"

Ester hid the book behind her back.

"I told you to give it to me," urged her mother.

Ester kept silent, her hand still clenching the book.

When her mother grabbed her arm and began to shout: "Let it go! Give it to me!" Ester dropped the book on the ground and yelled at her: "I was given this by the nuns!"

It was always like that between them. Her mother had never trusted her. She had never realised that there was nothing wrong with what she did.

With this conclusive thought, Ester felt her muscles relax. Her soft pillow was suddenly protective. Darkness was bliss. A moment later she was asleep.

Amalia was exhausted. It was always like that with her daughter. Why didn't she ever bend? Ester was always hard. Always ready to bite back. With all the work she did for her and for the entire family. That was how her sacrifices were rewarded! Amalia wanted to cry but she could not. Her dry eyes stung with rage. If only her daughter had realised that she was doing this for her own good.

She recalled when she was Ester's age. She saw the man she had loved. He had left her on the eve of their wedding. She had almost died of pain. Then Bepi arrived. The first thing she saw of him was his clear eyes, the innocent eyes of a man who knows no evil.

"I'm a painter," he had said a little distractedly. As if that was a trade! A job is what gives you bread. She knew it all too well, she who had worked hard every single day that God sent on earth. And it would go on like that as long as God willed.

The day was over. The café had closed. Sitting up in bed, Bepi was reading a book. She also went to bed, but she could not sleep, and after the light was off she kept hearing the sounds of shots fired on the river and vulgar laughter, and deep inside she felt the dull ache of not being understood.

Undzer Shtetl Brent

23rd May 1945, Lublin.

Silence in the hospital room. Distant footsteps in the corridor. Antonio had dozed all afternoon and was now awake. More awake than he had been in days. As awake as you can be only in a hospital ward, with all your senses alert and nothing deserving your attention.

"Hey, you're not sleeping?" murmured the man in the next bed, who was also Italian. Antonio shook his head. There was no need for compliments between those who had gone through what they had gone through.

"There's something I've been wanting to ask you for a few days. Are you a Jew?"

Antonio gave a start of surprise: "Why?"

"You know that I'm a Jew, don't you?"

Antonio shook his head again. "I knew you were a Jew, Alfredo, but why do you think...?"

"It's your last name. There's a rabbi called Ascari – Eleazar Ascari of Safed. He lived in Safed in the sixteenth century. It's a place on the top of a hill, near the lake of Tiberias."

"And what did this Ascari do?"

"He wrote a book. I've read it."

"Now I find that I am a Jew like you!"

"Maybe we're all Jews," said Alfredo.

"Maybe. Perhaps we don't know we are," Antonio answered with a smile.

"Perhaps you don't know."

"Listen. Do you think we'll make it?"

"I don't know. Your friend has fared well, right?"

"Yes, he's already out of the hospital. He's waiting to go back to Italy. But in my case..."

"Perhaps we should say: *God's will be done*, assuming that we still believe in God after what happened. And in what God then? Yours, mine, Allah? If God is one, then we are all Jews, and all Christians and all Muslims, no?"

"If God is one, then we are all brothers," said Antonio, "but I do not know if God exists. When I was young I did not worry about this. Now it seems too late."

"It's never too late. We're always inside. Inside God or inside the problem. There's no way out. We all have to deal with God."

"I think it is him who has to deal with us," said Antonio. "Don't you think he owes us an apology?"

"I think so. I don't know when we will meet him, but if it happens soon I intend to ask for it. We Jews talk a lot with God, as the Bible says. And we're good at bargaining. Do you remember how Abraham curbs the wrath of God when God wants to destroy Sodom and Gomorrah?"

"I don't remember. Yet, I should know, but it's been a few years since I last went to Mass..."

"Abraham tells God that perhaps in that city there are fifty righteous people. He will not want them to die along with the wicked! So where's the justice of God?

God thinks about it and agrees. If there are fifty righteous people, no punishment.

But Abraham raises the stake. What if the righteous people are not exactly fifty... Let's say that five of the fifty are lacking. The Lord will not want to sacrifice those righteous for lack of five?

The Lord is just, but Abraham is smart and the figures keep changing.

And if the righteous were forty? And if they were thirty? And if they were twenty?

And the Lord assents over and over again.

And if they were ten?

We Jews never give in. We always had to bargain with God to ensure our survival, and even now it is like that."

"But you wouldn't want to tell me that what is behind the Nazis is God's punishment? I've known too many Germans to look at it that way. Behind the Nazis there are only the Nazis. There's all the arrogance of our dear human beings, our indifference."

Antonio kept silent for a moment.

"When I was a kid I struck another child. He had red hair. He was the only boy in the class with red hair. And then he was skinny. He always sniffled. The easiest thing was to beat him. To show the others that I could. When I grew up I was ashamed."

"You see, you are better than the Nazis. In your eyes, how many of them feel ashamed?"

These words fell into silence.

"I don't know. I just know that if there's a God he forgives everyone, everyone."

Suddenly Antonio felt tired. He was tired of the weight of the last year. Tired of the distance from home, of hunger, of his suffering body.

He slipped into a deep and dreamless sleep.

22nd June 1945, Bologna.

"Veronica, you've come at last... I haven't seen you for months. How are you?"

"Well, Aunt Teresa. You must excuse me. I have brought Carlo... "

"The baby's here? Bring him to me. Let me touch him."

Veronica walked over to her aunt, who was sitting in the garden.

"Do you want to go to Aunt Teresa?" Veronica asked Carlo, but the question was addressed to the old woman.

"Yes, put him in my arms, the darling pet!"

Having entrusted Carlo to her aunt, Veronica stayed down on her knees, ready to intervene, but Carlo peacefully grabbed the old lady's finger.

"It's hot, huh?" murmured Veronica.

Antenesca brought a jug with sour cherry syrup. She asked Veronica if she could go to the grocery store while she was there.

Veronica was alone with her aunt. "How are you?"

"How do you think I am? I get along. In a week Antenesca is leading me to San Benedetto! You know that they have bombed everything, don't you? Of the church, only the walls remain. The cloister is no more. But they have patched up the house. Shortly, they want to take me there on holiday. Of course with the heat we have here in Bologna... for a poor blind woman like me it's torture. Always sitting here, doing nothing. At least there I can smell the countryside, listen to the birds.

"Now I live for these things. You have no idea how your life changes if your eyes are taken away from you. But you discover things that you had before and you didn't realise it. There are other ways of living, of being in the world. I don't mean flavours, since I've always been greedy, but smells for instance. I recognise them much more than before."

Veronica listened.

"Only, I've turned into such an ugly old crone. Without seeing I do not even know if my hair is combed. I almost do not know what I'm wearing."

"You're always the same, Aunt," said Veronica. "Do you remember that fur cape you had. The one with tails. You wore it above that dress with lace sleeves."

"Of course I remember."

"I thought you were beautiful! When I was a child I watched you. I wanted to be like you."

"Take the baby," said Teresa. "There's something I want to give you, you know! A small thing, but I know that you liked it. I spoke with Antenesca before. It is she who went to look for it."

When Veronica had Carlo in her arms, her aunt drew a pendant from her pocket. It was a cylinder of blue hard stone, mounted in gold, which turned on a pivot. The frame was all swirls and curls.

"When you were little you liked it so much. It has no value, eh, but I thought that you would be glad to have it. I hope it will bring you good luck and I wish you a better life than mine."

2nd July 1945, Lublin.

The two doctors standing by Antonio's bed exchanged a look that said more than words. The patient continued to worsen. They had seen so many go that way.

When the church clock struck a quarter past twelve Antonio asked for some water. It was the last water he drank. Half asleep, he drew a long breath, perhaps a sigh, then his muscles stretched.

Antonio was-and-was-not in the reflection of the sun on the ceiling,

he-was-and-was-not in the crunching of gravel in the yard,

he-was-and-was-not in the bright yellow of a dandelion,

he-was-and-was-not in the perfume of lindens,

he-was-and-was-not in the bouncing of a ball,

he-was-and-was-not in the flights of birds,

he-was-and-was-not...

he-was-and-was-not...

he-was-and-was-not.

3rd July 1945, Lublin.

In the morning when Antonio was buried a gentle wind blew. It blew under a clear sky, flecked with soft clouds. Those clouds were not menacing. It was a summer morning.

Alfredo's lungs were better, much better. Doctors and nuns agreed when he asked to accompany Antonio to that meadow on the outskirts of the city. In the hospital they had shared something. He had to be there on that day. He could not leave him alone.

He was walking in the open air for the first time after the weeks he had spent in bed, after the long time of imprisonment, of absolute suffering, of absolute indifference. At one point he felt tired and asked to sit on the handcart that was carrying Antonio.

He felt the wind touch his face. It seemed so strange. It blew from the south-west. Over there – perhaps two miles away? – was the Majdanek camp, which had been abandoned for almost a year, since the arrival of the Soviets in Lublin.

How many people? How many hundreds of people? How many thousands of people? How many hundreds of thousands of people had died in that camp?

Alfredo felt overwhelmed. He looked at the open meadow towards the countryside and he imagined all those dead people standing there. He would have liked to approach them.

All of a sudden, the wind carried them away. In front of him only a hole remained, into which a body was being lowered, wrapped in a sheet.

A friend. He had found a friend. He could not recite the *Kaddish*. There was no *minyan* of ten men. He did not have a *kippah* on his head. There was not even a dead Jew in front of him.

For a moment it seemed to him that in that place at that time he had nothing to grasp. The chilled wind of the winters he had gone through, the nights he had gone through, the beatings and the hatred, had taken everything away from him. He had no tears left to cry. He had no hopes or desires. He did not have a family. He did not have a home.

Then he saw the earth fall into the pit and cover three white sheets. He saw those men who were toiling to bury three lifeless bodies. And he knew that there was something he could cling to. Compassion.

We are all Jews. God has given the promised land to all mankind, to Isaac and Ishmael. In that holy blasphemy Alfredo felt alive. As long as there was another man in the world – as long as he could look into the eyes of somebody and be looked at – he could continue to be a Jew and to pray to God for the salvation of all his children.

20th July 1945, Novara.

Pina opened the wardrobe and looked at her husband's clothes. She touched them with her hand. She savoured the material of a jacket with her fingers, she buried her face in its collar and shoulders. He would never use those clothes any more. It was all over.

She had received a message from Lublin. A cold official statement. Then the letter had arrived and she had finally been able to cry. She kept it in the drawer, along with the letters he wrote to her before they got married, along with the cards he had sent her from Germany. She had copied it and sent it to her mother-in-law. And when she had finished she had started to cry.

Her mother did not know how to comfort her, but it had to be so. There was no other way. There was only a big black pain, like a dull fog she had to cross. She did not know what was beyond that pain, but her heart did not show her any other way.

She went to church and could not pray. She gave piano lessons to children and her head was elsewhere. She spoke with her mother and answered at random.

She thought of consulting a medium. She could not believe that she would not see him again. Never again. Those words tormented her soul. They rang in her ears, piercing her eardrums and her temples, and emerged from her eyes in the form of tears.

It was one of the harder days. Outside it was raining. It was hot though and the window was open. Suddenly she heard music, a rhythm. She turned to look for someone, but the room was empty. There was only that rhythmic sound.

She looked out of the window. On the pavement that ran around the house, a large flower pot was filled with water. From the downspout. She could see the drops falling from above, falling and drawing circles in the water. Circles like music...

As soon as the music reached her, she ran to the piano. It was like a wind blowing from her hands. The instrument was her body, her body the instrument.

Her hands touched the keys with a lover's delicacy. The hammers were dying of sweetness while caressing the strings. Her foot pursued the impossible desire to merge with the smooth, rounded metal of the pedal. The felts muffled sounds as two faces close in a kiss.

Then the music changed. It began to swell with the months of waiting, with the sleepless nights, with her inability to accept, with the happiness of others, with her agonizing fate, with the white-hot rage and the despair that was freezing inside her.

When the storm melted into a sad certainty, that note remained. A melancholy and gentle note... A note that would never yield. The melody regained its sweetness: the sweetness of love, the sweetness of memory.

All of a sudden, she realised she was happy, because she was with him again in the music that he loved, that she had taught him to love.

She wept as she played. She cried with joy and pain. She railed against the war that had taken him away right at the end, when it was time to return. But every life has its design, its rhythm. The music is written and we can only play, play and feel, feel and play.

Those five black lines she had before her, that fragment of life that a man of distant times had put on paper one day, no one could steal from her. That drop of water that fell and fell and fell once again, insistent and intoxicating, had become music. His music. Her music. Music would help her live and regain her Antonio.

21st July 1945, Loiano.

Dear Ester,

Today at last we received a recent letter from you. I hasten to thank you and to respond that we are in good health. As soon as postal services were re-established, I wrote several times giving you our news. We also had a letter posted by some friends of ours who live in Bolzano, hoping that you would receive our news more easily, but as I gather from your letter nothing has reached you yet. I repeat, therefore, in brief what I had written in full. We have now had many letters from Giulio, both old and very recent ones. He keeps asking for you assuring that he has written to you quite often, but he has never received any answers. He was in France for six months, and he is now in Germany. His address remains the following:

Ascari Giulio Sergeant Major 81 – I – 9908

7169 Laundry Co. Ital.

U.S. Army. P.W.I.B – France

Despite the bombings and the rain of grenades that kept us wide awake for seven months, a part of our house has miraculously survived, while much of the village was destroyed.

On 5th April I had a child. Carlo is now on my knees distracting me with his little movements, preventing me from writing correctly.

You will therefore forgive me if my letter is messy. Together with Mummy, who always remembers you, I am sending the most dear and affectionate thoughts to you and your family.

Affectionately,
Veronica

26th July 1945, Loiano.

Maria felt so old. She had never felt so old. When news of Antonio had reached her, it was as if an invisible hand had struck her.

She had not recovered yet. She had not regained her balance. She walked with difficulty. She leaned on tables, on walls. And she was just over sixty!

She read and re-read the letter that Pina had copied for her, the letter in which a fellow prisoner of Antonio described their days in a Polish hospital:

With Antonio, we entered the hospital at the end of April. We were both struck by pneumonia while crossing the front. No one could help us or move us because there were neither hospitals nor means of transport. So we had to make do with the help of some good friends and after a long journey we managed to reach Lublin. As a consequence the disease was neglected and worsened, notably in the case of your husband. After ten days I walked out of hospital, free of pneumonia, but two months later he was still suffering. The agony of that journey aggravated his condition despite the continuous diligent care of physicians and nuns, and of those of us who had recovered our health (after leaving hospital I brought him what he needed). A nurse who was also descended from an Italian family did everything she could and brought him everything she could.

I left on 19th June and I implored her to take the greatest care of him. Rest assured that she cared for him like a mother.

On 19th June, dear Antonio was not very well. Yet, his case was not hopeless. Up to the 10th he got out of bed by himself. After that date he needed to be tended in bed. Let me tell you, however, that they treated him kindly, as a dear son.

Every time she read the letter, at this point she began to cry. As if she was again forced to separate from him. Perhaps it was because of that last line: *they treated him kindly, as a dear son.*

Where was she when it happened? What was she doing? What was she thinking? Why, Lord, at that time she could not know and pray and cry and tear her hair and die together with that son who had died before her?

She still had Giulio – Giulio, who had not come home yet. She had to pray for him. She would think of him all the time. Even at night she would pray. She would not let God take him away from her while she looked away.

28th August 1945, Travesio.

Dear Giulio,

At last I received a letter you wrote a month ago. This gives me hope that mine will also reach you. I am so glad to know you are fine, just sad that I cannot see you yet. My fellow townsmen who were detained far away have all come back and this anxious waiting in vain brings me great pain.

You cannot imagine how many things I have to tell you. I won't even begin now because I believe that this would do you more harm than good. By pure chance Daddy and I are still alive. I refrain from telling you what would read like a novel. I am so anxious to hear from you about your life during these five eternal and short years.

Do your best to come back. I am dying of desire to see you again. Although your Ester still feels like a child, in particular for you, she is almost twenty-four, and when she marries you she wants her dowry to consist of her youth, not of her spinsterhood.

Do the possible and the impossible to come back if you do not want to increase my suffering.

Your family and I are always corresponding. You can thank God that they too are alive.

I think you've guessed what a surprise awaits you. Are you happy? I guess your Mother is as happy as Veronica and Cleto.

This year I applied for a job near Pordenone, I hope I will get it. I spent two weeks in Venice. I would love to go back with you. Please, if you cannot come, at least write to me every day. My family, who rejoice every time one of your letters arrives, greet you, hoping to see you soon.

I am sending you a thousand kisses so that you know how big my love is,

Your Ester

5th September 1945, Travesio.

Bepi returned to his stream, where the water touched the blue of the sky, the bright green of the leaves. That stream which was always the same and always different. Water. The origin of life. The image of life with its relentless flow.

Life went on. War was over. Gone were the days of the empire. As if they had not had enough land around them! And the most beautiful land in the world.

Bepi was not a patriot. He was a painter. He loved the land for what it was. He had no need for flags and borders. The land belonged to everyone. It fed the body and the soul with its fruits and its beauty.

Bepi took out his pipe. Beside him, his colour-box remained closed. He did not feel like painting. He was happy contemplating. He sat watching the water that flowed in that stretch of river, which spread to form a small lake, upstream of a curving dam, at the mouth of the narrow channel that led to the mill.

Life went on, although so many had died in war. Death. He was not afraid of it. He saw himself, after his death, flying to the places he loved, lighter and happier than he now was, at one with the wind, with water, playing among the rocks, among the foliage. He saw himself as liquid. Without bones. Without form. At one with all forms. One in one.

But he was there, alive. It was the others who had learned what dying means. Dying for a just cause and dying for a wrong cause. What a sad fate! Because ideas remained. Good ideas and bad ones. Those for which it was worth dying and those he regarded as wrong, deeply wrong.

Yet all lives had their value. Each life had a value. He was thinking of all those lives that could have been saved. He was suffering for all those lives that had ended in a tragic mistake. What an immense waste.

Love for the world. There was no love for the world. He felt like crying for the pain of this awareness, for all the blood that had been spilled, for all the faces that he would never see again.

There remained in him a sad consciousness of evil. And along with it a desire to be reunited with nature, in which he found his inspiration. Because his paintings were for him a form of experience. The experience of the air that caressed his skin as he painted on spring days, the water reflections that played on his face as he sat on the bank of the stream. The fresh smell of the water in the shadow of the trees, for water had a smell. Space. The horizontality of meadows, the verticality of mountains, the geometry of valleys, the immensity of skies. The sense of being surrounded by an intensity of life, by forces that were beyond the human.

He went to church on a Sunday, but he had not met God there. He had met him in the fields where the corn cobs grew, in the path that crossed a wood, opening into a clearing that was drenched with light. He had met him in his river, in the blue profile of the peaks that embraced the horizon.

The war was over. Pain remained. Above all else, life remained. Ideas also remained, both the right and the wrong ones, and all those dead to mourn. They had to build a new country, a better country. They had to keep all those dead in their hearts.

The pipe had gone out. He set it on the ground and slowly opened the box that contained his colours.

Back Home

8th October 1945, Loiano.

My dear Ester,

I am writing to you from home where I finally arrived last night after three long years.

I want to reassure you immediately that I am still thinking about you as I have been during the long and sad days of captivity.

Of course I very much wish to see you again and I plan to come to Travesio as soon as possible. Here I found my dear ones well but our house and land in very bad condition. Everything has been devastated by war. In my following letters, and as soon as I can speak with you on the phone, I will tell you everything. I hope your family are well, and I urge you to greet them affectionately on my part. A warm hug and a tender kiss from your

Giulio

15th October 1945, Loiano.

When Giulio came home from the war, he claimed he had had a lot of fun. As a prisoner of the Americans he had been promoted to head chef and had always had wonderful meals. His mother noticed that he had picked up strange habits. He spread

149

steaks with jam because Americans eat them like that. And then he smoked and smoked. It seemed that Americans had given them all the cigarettes they wanted. He had been playing cards and draughts with the other prisoners for hours. He had been lucky to end up with the Americans!

Maria could not believe that she had him back with her. With everything that had happened, at least her youngest son, the son who had been closer to her, the one she had sheltered from life when his father... Giulio was there! At night she did things that she would have been ashamed to tell. Sometimes she woke up and to be certain that it was true, that he had really come back, she went to the door of his room. She heard his light snore and then she was happy. She went back to bed, and slept peacefully.

At other times she dreamed of Antonio, always as a child. Once it was a terrible dream. Antonio's voice was calling her. A cry of anguish, full of fear. She looked for him in every room, but she could not find him, until in her dream she remembered he was dead. She awoke with a start. She decided that she would build him a grave in the village cemetery. Although he was buried in faraway Poland, he would have his tomb in Loiano. At least she would know where to go and pray, where to bring flowers, where to think of him.

26th March 1946, Travesio.

Dear Giulio,

I was sad the other night to write you such a short and messy letter. You must excuse me, my darling. I think it is the first I have sent you of that kind. Here we have no good news. Masked and armed people knock on people's doors asking for money. In addition to this we have the fortune to host Slavs. Rumour has it that they are in the mountains. Since I heard that I have lost my peace of mind. It seems to me we are going back to the dark times.

Apart from this, life is not so bad. I like my job at school, and when I am at home I spend my time doing small jobs. Sometimes I take a little bike ride or a walk in the countryside. Now days go by fast enough. My every action has only one aim. I look at new dress designs, I visit shops. Everything concerning my marriage and our future is important to me. I always think about what can make me nice in your eyes, and what I can do to keep the heart of my love close to me. When I receive your news the sun starts shining.

Your last letter was dated the 19th, the one before was dated the 16th. You write every third day. What does this mean? Are you just lazy?

When you come here, I will hardly have time to give you all the kisses that I have sent you. However I keep sending you a lot. Add them to my tally, and don't worry: sooner or later I'll pay all my debts. A big hug to you and your Mum.

Your Ester

6th April 1946, Travesio.

Why had she gone? Perhaps to save her parents that sight? Perhaps for an obscure desire to relive her hours of anguish? To cross the threshold between life and death? To try the impossible experience of what might have happened? The fact was on that morning it was Ester who climbed the mountain, together with her two orphaned cousins, to identify the body of her aunt, which had been thrown, together with others, in a *foiba*, a sink hole, one of the many natural chasms that marked the region.

On that April morning, as she walked along with the men, everything was the same and everything was different from an October morning now far away and yet always close.

They had brought a sheet with them. They followed the path between the rocks and the grass, which was still brown and dry up there. When Ester looked up, she saw a V-shaped stone valley and behind it the sky. Against the intense, almost electric blue, a white and light grey cloud, as neat as if it had been painted, was swollen with new life. The mountain was still asleep, but the sky announced the incipient spring.

They climbed and climbed on that steep path, and no one spoke. Suddenly the *carabiniere* who escorted them said: "This is the spot."

They had arrived at a plateau, halfway up the mountain. There was nothing around, apart from scattered boulders, rocks jutting from the ground, tufts of leafless shrubs. They walked on a bed of dried up ferns that had been crushed by snow. After a few steps, Ester noticed a depression in the ground. Following the *carabiniere*, she and her cousins approached what looked like a hole at the centre of the basin. Leaning on a rock, Ester bent slightly forward, as if afraid of what she might see, but there was nothing to see. Down there, it was still night.

"The sink hole goes down more than eighty metres. They came all the way from Trieste to bring out the bodies. They have been working since the early morning. They had to throw down three rope ladders thirty metres each to go down."

Ester knew that there were eleven bodies, including five women. She hugged her younger cousin with an abrupt gesture that was meant to be nice. Perhaps it was the first time he was, for her, in the first place a person, a human being to whom she directly related, not an unfortunate child her mother took care of while crying about the fate of his parents.

The two cousins were silent. Ester was silent. The policeman gestured with his hand: "They're here. If you want to come with me. They started with the women."

Lined up behind a rock, in a small meadow, were those miserable remains of a life. Torn, ragged clothes. Ghosts of colours. Twisted hair. Perhaps faces. Hands and legs.

Ester did not dare to approach. No, this time it was modesty that restrained her. She left her two cousins to look for the remains of their mother: the boy who was a child only yesterday, and his elder brother, who was by now sixteen. A silent young man, whose rage was imprisoned down there.

The two brothers would leave for Australia a short time later. They would make it to a distant land drenched in sunshine. To escape the attraction of the black hole ~~~~ ~~~ uld follow them in their d~ The time would come for ~ g their thirst for revenge, ~

Did~ico Centennial 416-394-5330 had recognised her? Th~ronto Public Library ~ was closed. A few na~ ~d of a body, a memer ID: 2 ********** 1086

I~Date Format: DD/MM/YYYY   ~ite, shapeless thoug ~ the verge of sting~Number of Items: 1   into the *foibe* whil~ Item ID:37131177204153 ped.

Title:Faded letters
Date due:02/02/2017

She saw him
wa ~is knees. The
yo   Telephone Renewal# 416-395-5505   is brother – a
big   www.torontopubliclibrary.ca   ry. He felt the
wo   Thursday, January 12, 2017 5:20 PM

was all over.
Mu   ~mbrace him
aga

ran towards
his ~ ~ardly knew.
He ~   . . .   ~~~ was not his

mother, someone who looked at the world with new eyes, like him, without possessing its secret.

The little brother ran up to the big one and touched his shoulder from behind and the big brother turned to his little brother and his eyes had filled with tears, and – for the first time – he took him in his arms and his face flooded with love. The love that had to find a way to rise to the surface, unless hate took its place. Then the two brothers loved each other and that bond would never be broken because it was born as a bridge over the chasm that had opened beneath them.

They resumed their journey back. The big brother decided that they would carry the coffin. He who was tall and strong, in front, and his little brother behind, along with a *carabiniere.* They wanted to accompany their mother as if that made her path sweeter, as if to undo the spell of the journey that had led her alone to death.

Ester did not know what to do. She did not know what to say. She did not know if she had done well to come with them that day. She thought and thought, and paid much attention to where she was placing her feet, for she knew that a breath of wind, a slight emotion, would suffice to make her fall.

She saw her aunt coming up the path, but she was thinking of a younger woman, who had gone up another path, and from the mountain had come back alive. Large drops began to fall from the grey sky. She heard them hit the wooden coffin. They went down her face like tears, but she was not crying.

Suddenly she thought of Giulio and said to herself: *I want a baby.*

16th June 1946, Loiano.

The bells were already ringing. The first Sunday Mass was about to begin, but that day Maria was not ready.

"He says he will throw himself out of the window! He says he's a failure. 'I'm a failure! I'm thirty-one, and I don't even have a job!' He was screaming like a madman. What should I do?"

"Oh, Mum. Giulio has always been like that. What did he say when you enrolled him in the course for radio operators, in Livorno? He couldn't hear the interval between signals. And in the end he didn't graduate! Then there was the war. Just imagine: finding a job now is not easy."

"I'll tell you one thing, but you must promise me not to tell anyone and not to get angry. He thinks he will live off his property. The other day he said I'll have to leave everything to him because he's the most needy. And then: 'If I cannot marry Ester I'll kill myself!' He made a scene. I don't know which way to take him, Veronica. Would you like two eggs? The hens have just laid them!"

"Thank you, Mum. I'll take them for Carlo."

"Well, Veronica. Now I have to go to Mass."

29th January 1947, Travesio.

For Ester's wedding, all her relatives were there. Even Aunt Gina came from Vicenza. Only Cleto had come from Bologna. He would act as a witness. Given the condition of the roads and railways, one could hardly expect Veronica to travel with a small child, or Giulio's mother to embark on such a long journey.

Amalia worked for days on the refreshments. Finding good things was not easy, but she was full of resources. She closed the café that Monday to celebrate the newly-weds.

Ester's cousin Gianni had offered to take pictures. Everybody posing outside the church, then only the bride and groom as they descended the steps, then the bride with her mother. Once at home, Gianni was continually taking photographs. Twenty people were sitting around the table and he kept snapping and snapping.

"Enough of these photos. How much will they cost?" Amalia said to her nephew, but he would not listen: "Money and I don't get along well. We always part quickly! Put your arm round Mum so that I can take a picture of you two."

Courses followed one other to the applause and cheers of guests. When the time came to cut the cake, someone invited the new couple to exchange a kiss.

Ester went all red, but Giulio embraced her at the waist, screening her with his face. They looked like movie stars. "He's a handsome boy," said Aunt Tilde to Aunt Lidia. "She's just beautiful!" answered Lidia, who started crying every five minutes.

The time came to leave for Udine. The next morning they would go on by train to Venice. Ester was happy. She knew Venice, thanks to her uncle Memi, but going there on her honeymoon was another matter entirely. She would discover the gondolas and outdoor cafés.

They all came out to greet Ester and Giulio. The newly-weds had already entered the car along with Cleto, who would take a train from Udine, when Gianni came up with a sly smile: "Don't sleep late tomorrow," he said, and you could see he was repressing a laugh.

Once in Udine, the driver stopped in front of a shabby-looking little hotel. It was Gianni who had booked the room.

The man at the entrance took a key and invited them to follow him. Ester walked with her handbag under her arm and a bag in which she had put her wedding dress. She wanted to have it in her new home. Giulio brought the two suitcases.

The room was an attic, but in those days you had to be content.

They were dead tired. Ester only wanted to get her shoes off. She made to sit down, but under her weight half of the bed crashed onto the floor.

A brief inspection told Giulio that two legs had been sawn off. No doubt the joker was Gianni... Ester did not know whether to laugh or cry. They slept tight in the other half of the bed.

The real surprise was still to come. For another joke, Gianni had taken all the photos of the wedding without film.

1st February 1947, Bologna.

Their two days in Venice had flown. The first thing Ester and Giulio did when they got off the train was to visit Aunt Teresa. It was she who had asked.

Antenesca came to the door. "I'll turn on the light," she said before they entered the old lady's room, which was on the ground floor. *She spends her time in the dark,* Ester thought, *as if she was already in the grave.* This made her feel uneasy. Then she realised that the blind do not care about light. And when that fat woman rose from her chair and Ester saw her open smile, she forgot that first fear, that sense of closure.

A little later, they were eating Antenesca's *ciambella* cake and Aunt Teresa was joking and Ester already felt a little more at home.

As they left, she saw a photo on the mantelpiece. There was a priest sitting on a chair. Standing next to him was a boy in uniform, wearing his hat. A smaller boy was sitting on the knee of the priest. Behind them a painted backdrop: the sea, plants, a column.

Ester said nothing. She knew that Giulio's cousin was in an asylum.

When they were in the street, she asked Giulio, "That picture above the fireplace: was it your cousin?"

"The two boys are Antonio and Francesco. They were in boarding school. To think that one is buried in Poland and the other is in Imola..." Giulio shook himself, as if he had just remembered the most important thing in the world: "We have to look for some flowers for Veronica! Let's buy them now. She doesn't live far away. Down there on the avenue."

"Flowers in February? And it's almost dark."

"Then let's take some pastries. Of course with these suitcases..."

Ester looked up and laughed: "Look over there where the pastry shop is. Right in front of your aunt's house!"

22nd June 1947, Loiano.

The Mille Miglia had not passed through Loiano since 1938, since that terrible accident in Bologna and the government had cancelled the race. Instead of the Mille Miglia, in 1940 they had organized the Grand Prix of Brescia, but it was not the same. However, after the war began nobody talked about motor racing any more.

For this reason, when the Mille Miglia was reinstated – the evening of 21st June 1947 – people rejoiced. The war was really over, even if the signs of devastation were everywhere. Many of the bridges over the Po had been blown up, making it necessary to change the route. For the first time the race was run in a clockwise direction and passed through Bologna only once, after crossing the Apennines.

When the cars arrived at the Albergo Pellegrino, a sea of people was waiting for them. Ester was standing next to Giulio, who told her the racers' names and introduced her to some of his acquaintances. Someone made a comment about the past and Giulio remembered that day long ago when the Mille Miglia first passed through Loiano. He thought of his brother. He almost felt Antonio was there with them.

Raindrop Prelude

6th April 1950, Loiano.

Giulio did not have a car. And then he had to work. They had asked Ariodante to pick Pina up. When she arrived at the station, at around half past four, she did as she had been told. Coming out of the main hall, she found the portico where she was to wait.

The fat, placid man was leaning against the last column.

She did not have time to ask "Are you Signor Ariodante?" before he had taken off his hat and had grabbed her suitcase. He had a grey FIAT 1100.

"What a nice car!" she said with her Piedmont accent, and Ariodante replied in Bolognese: "A little gem!"

As they drove along the streets, they talked of reconstruction. The city was changing, but there were still lots of refugees.

"You know, Signora, in front of the stadium here in Bologna there is a long arcade. It takes you to the cemetery, which is called Certosa. Well, during the war they closed the arches with brick walls and lived there. Some people still live there! There are refugees everywhere. It's hard! They live on nothing."

In the meantime, Pina looked around. There was so much desolation, but life went on. The façade of a house in ruins was covered with large posters: *senza pietà* UN FILM LUX, *senza pietà* UN FILM LUX, *senza pietà* UN FILM LUX. Beside it a new building was under construction. It must have been seven or eight floors! The trams were running on their thin rails. Bikes, trucks, children clutching their mothers' hands – she was moved by everything she saw in that city.

A riot police van passed by. She was afraid of them. She had seen too many uniforms. How long would it take to rebuild? She felt tired.

The car fled the city. Here were the hills. She saw villages that she had crossed in the course of a previous life. Rastignano. Carteria di Sesto. Pianoro was still an expanse of ruins, although the first new houses were sprouting from that desolation. She could not believe her eyes. How much destruction!

Ariodante had stopped talking. He was intent on driving on that road that was now all climbs and bends. It began to rain. The drops rolled down the windows. The trees and fields, outside, were the same as always. She almost felt transported to a different time, as if there had been nothing. She could have brought... But no, she already had many gifts.

She would see her mother-in-law and Giulio, and she would get to know Ester. And she would see little Lisetta, who was by now a year old! How much time had gone by. She felt old, and again she fell prey to that sense of exhaustion.

Ariodante resumed talking. He told her about the restaurant in Zula, where they ate good *tagliatelle* and people came all the way from Bologna. He told her about the growing traffic. There were more and more trucks on the road. It was good for Loiano because that meant new shops and petrol stations and restaurants. The road meant prosperity for Loiano!

Meanwhile, the landscape became more familiar. At times it stopped raining, then it started again. She recognised Livergnano, Sabbioni. They were almost there.

When they approached the village, she saw the house on the left. At first it seemed to her that everything was the same, also because of the trees. Then, when they took the climb to get into the yard, she realised. Half of the house was gone. They had quickly built a barn on the ruins, against the turret.

While Ariodante preceded her with her suitcase in his hand, the door was already opening She saw a young woman with a baby in her arms. Pina loved children. She would have liked one.

She felt that on that trip, on that day, death and life were before her, but life was calling. Coming out of the torpor that had cradled her in the car, Pina found the strength to say: "You must be little Lisetta! Then this must be your mother, Ester..."

After dinner, she retired to her room. Only then did she realise how tired she was. Seeing her mother and brother-in-law. Going back to that house. Antonio's room had been destroyed. They put her in a bedroom that she did not remember, next to that of Ester and Giulio. She only longed to sleep.

Waking up in the night, she did not realise where she was.

She held out her hand towards her bedside table and lamp, but she found nothing. She was afraid. As if the world had changed in the darkness that surrounded her. She lacked support. She almost fell from bed.

Then she remembered her journey, her arrival and her stern mother-in-law, who had not been able to say a word of affection. She thought of her husband, who had played as a child in those rooms. She thought of the books he had read, that he had told her about. Of the races he had run in the meadows round there.

She had not cried for a long time. Sometimes crying had done her good, but that night her crying was only suffering, sobs that pain tore out of her like gagging. Spasms of anger.

No, no, no! Why did it have to happen to her? Why *her*? In the darkness that surrounded her, only a big, harsh denial. She could not, she would not, she should not accept it. No. No. No. *Why did you have to die? Why aren't you here? Why can't we be happy?*

As soon as these thoughts rose from deep down inside her, Pina threw them back again into the black hole where they emerged again in the shape of tears. Tears which corroded her eyes and cheeks, which stiffened her muscles. And she kept weeping and sobbing, and perhaps she had also shouted. She never knew how long it lasted.

Suddenly she was so tired that she fell back into a slumber, surrounded by a deep silence.

In the next room Ester was listening. In her sleep she had heard a groan. She thought of her daughter, but the girl was sleeping peacefully beside her. Her mother-in-law? She slept away from the young couple. Another moan, the sound of crying. Ester at last understood. It came from the room next to them. Poor woman.

Ester felt her heart tighten and reopen. She wanted to go. She had to go. But she was afraid of making a mistake. What would her husband say? He was there. He kept sleeping. And her mother-in-law? How could she go? She, who was not even part of the family? They had just met. If *they* were not going, how could *she* go?

She would always regret it. Not having got up that night. Not having entered the next room without knocking. Not having embraced that lonely unhappy woman.

But she did not move. She kept clinging to her sheets – frozen by shame and terror – until that painful crying ended and silence was restored. Silence, she hoped, would restore sleep, but sleep shuns cowards. She lay there curled up, feeling a cold that came from inside her.

She reached out to find her husband, but she did not want to wake him. She put her hand on his back, gently, to feel his warmth, to prove that it was true, that she was not the other woman, that her life was warm with love. And she prayed to God to forgive her for her silence and to help those who had to suffer so much. And then she fell asleep.

She heard her husband get out of bed to go to work. It was time to make breakfast. She rose.

In two days it would be Easter. She would make a nice cake with coloured butter cream – a little pink cream, with *alchermes* liqueur, a little brown cream, with chocolate, and a little white one, just butter and sugar. She would prepare it in front of Pina, so she could learn how to make it. It was a dessert that her Mum used to make.

22nd December 1968, Loiano.

I still remember that evening, waiting for her arrival. The light on the kitchen table. To pass the time, Dad had brought the plastic deck chairs into the room that in summer were on the balcony. On their chrome frame ran little plastic tubes – one green, the other orange. With two chairs and a blanket we had built an Indian hut.

I was in the middle of the Wild West when the doorbell rang. Mummy was back from Bologna. It was she who had gone to the station to fetch her, with Ariodante driving.

I remember the bell ringing and me running to open the door, and the lights in the sitting room, and that cheerful lady, wearing a fur cap. She played the song of the seven dwarfs on the piano, and I, who was three, I was happy.

I do not remember anything else about that night and the days to come. Years later, while I was running through my mother's piano scores, I found an album leaf: *Frédéric Chopin, Prelude Op. 28 (1839) no. 15 in D. Raindrop*. At the top right, on the opening page, a name and a date: *For Ester from Pina, Christmas 1968*. We would never see Aunt Pina again. A short time later, in Novara, a coach ran her over while it was reversing.

In the beginning

21st October 2010, Bologna.

Dear Dr Begozzi,

Following my phone call yesterday, when I inquired about Antonio Ascari, a resident of Novara at the time of World War II, who was deported to Germany as a textile technician on 1 March 1944, I am writing to correct some information I gave you.

The card that Uncle Antonio wrote from his place of imprisonment on May 20, 1944 did not come from Heidelberg, but from Werneuchen (2). The exact address is FlugplatzKommando A44/III Werneuchen (2) – Berlin.

Enclosed with this card was a view of Heidelberg. Perhaps the postcard, depicting a charming city with flowering trees, was aimed to distract the relatives' attention from the real conditions in his prison.

In the hope that you can give me some news of my uncle, thank you again for your kindness.

Sincerely,

Maurizio Ascari

21st October 2010, Novara, Institute for the History of the Resistance.

I respond promptly because yesterday, intrigued by your phone call, I immediately searched in the name archive. As I feared, without success.

The concentration camp universe comprised "infinite" categories of deportees and the real challenge today is not that of determining numbers and quantity, of the "drowned and the saved," as Primo Levi said, to define a phenomenon and its devastating complexity, but that of determining individual paths in the belief that every man and woman, although they were overwhelmed by the same destiny, was unique and unrepeatable.

This is also the meaning of our research, which starts therefore from the field, from the territories of origin of each person, from their pre- and possibly post-field experience.

That's why I was very intrigued by your phone call. When we started, without worrying too much about defining deportees (political, racial, homosexuals, or just slaves, etc.) we had a hundred names. Today we have identified over 400 with stories that are very different from one another, and at the same time terribly similar.

The archival references are often contradictory and the research paths are very difficult.

Had your uncle been a military man, I would have bet on an archive in Berlin, had he been a politician or a Jew or a gypsy, on Arolsen (CRI) or on the lists of transports. But since he was just a "worker", who had been more or less forced, things get complicated.

However, the municipal archives sometimes retain traces, notably from the aftermath, for example when families made inquiries.

I cannot promise a lot from this periphery (which is also an archival periphery), but I can attempt to make some soundings. Who knows? Perhaps in the end something will come to light.

This is why I am asking you to give me all the information in your possession (personal data, names of companies where he worked, how his family got to know about his death, by whom, etc.). Even small, apparently meaningless traces can open up avenues of research, something that you are aware of, given your job.

Again, I do not know what I can actually do, but if I can I will be happy to help you.

Best wishes
Mauro Begozzi

The postcards Antonio sent from Werneuchen are the only relics of the time he spent in Germany. I have not been able to find further information about his whereabouts. Who knows in what prison camp Antonio was interned. I do not know and I cannot picture him in a real camp. His prison is for me in Werneuchen. That is the place where he spent his captivity, in a camp that does not exist but that is all camps, irrespective of the actual place where fate cast him.

Acknowledgements

We tend to think of writing as an individual activity, but the longer I live the more I realise that writing is actually a communal effort. I have managed to complete this narrative thanks to the help of friends, and even of persons I have never met. Thanking them for the time they devoted to this text is both my duty and my pleasure. Yet, the fact that I am mentioning them in connection with this story does not mean that I am shifting in any way the responsibility of what I have written from my shoulders to theirs. Many people helped me along the way, opening my eyes to the shortcomings of what I had written or to narrative developments I had not fully explored, but it was I who made the final choices. Yet, it was only thanks to the generosity of those who shared this experience with me that I was able to go on. It was they who provided me with the energy I needed to shape this story.

A big thanks to all those who read (and sometimes patiently re-read) the Italian version, or better one of the many Italian versions, of this book, sharing their comments with me: Mauro Begozzi, Mirella Billi, Alessandra Calanchi, Maria Teresa Cassini, Alessandro Castellari, Remo Ceserani, Diana Kaley, Laura Falqui, Paolo Ferrucci, Annalisa Longega, Barnaba Maj, Ilaria Micheletti, Rita Monticelli, Eugenio Nascetti, Elisabetta Risari, Adriano Simoncini and Monica Turci. I have found your help invaluable!

A special thanks to the friends who helped me bridge the gap between my native Italian and English – a language I deeply love but which will never entirely lose its aura of mystery in my foreign eyes... It is thanks to the patience, dedication and creativity of Patricia Borlenghi, Philip Platts and Michael Webb that this text can now be read in fluent English, not in the stumbling patois that characterised my first draft translation.

I wish to thank Patricia Borlenghi warm-heartedly for accepting to publish this book. Had she not generously responded to this story, *Faded Letters* would be quietly resting in the proverbial drawer, or better in today's electronic equivalent of it, a computer file... Instead of an epitaph, this text has a title thanks to her decision to launch Patrician Press.

Moreover, this book has a cover thanks to Tim Roberts, who very kindly allowed us to use one of his linocuts.

It is now the turn of my family. Had they reacted jealously or suspiciously to my attempt to tell this story, my itinerary would have been very difficult, but that was not the case. Right from the beginning, I was encouraged by them to pursue the enterprise of tackling past events by means of fiction. When my text finally circulated within the family, it triggered a warm emotional response and my attempt at story-telling started to acquire a meaning. Stories live only insofar as they are read. Unless you feel the sympathy of some (prospective) readers, it is hard to keep striving to achieve a result.

Franca. She is at the origin of all my enterprises. She is the one who nurtures my ideas, providing me with the time and mental freedom that are necessary for the development of thought. Our intellectual and emotional exchanges are an endless source of energy for me. She is an ideal companion in every adventure and no words can express my gratitude. Franca has taught me what generosity and openness and love mean. No thank you will be big enough to repay my debt.